SPIZZERINCTUM

The Life and Legend of Robert "Black Bob" Renfro

By

Larry Michael Ellis

First published by AuthorHouse 06/03/04

ISBN: 1-4184-0848-4 (e-book)
ISBN: 1-4184-0849-2 (Paperback)
ISBN: 1-4184-0850-6 (Dust Jacket)

This book is printed on acid free paper.

Library of Congress Control Number: 2004092326

Printed in the United States of America
Bloomington, IN

ACKNOWLEDGEMENTS

I give thanks and recognition to the employees at the Tennessee State Archives, Montgomery County Archives, Robertson County Archives, Kingsport Public Library, Nashville-Davidson County Public Library, and special thanks to Debie Cox at the Nashville-Davidson County Archives. Without their patient assistance in directing a novice searcher through their treasure houses, this story would not have been possible. Also, special thanks to Nancy Sartor, a co-worker and author, who encouraged me to write the story.

I also thank Phillip L. Blake, soldier and scholar, who graciously consented to do the initial editing of my rough draft, turning it into a manuscript. Without his spelling and punctuation corrections, as well as his advice, this story may not have materialized. So too I thank my daughter Merci E. Chartrand, a language arts teacher, who polished the manuscript and mildly coerced me into making changes until it reached its final form.

And, lastly, I thank my wife of over 40 years, Linda, who continues to have faith in me.

DEDICATION

I am a sixth generation Tennessean.
I dedicate this book to those who have
gone before me and those who will come after.
But most of all to my parents,

Edward and Omega Ellis

Great Americans, who were born and raised in
Clarksville, Montgomery County, Tennessee.

PREFACE

Robert "Black Bob" Renfro is a real person in Tennessee history. Most details of Bob's life are not known; however, Bob's name appears in official records numerous times at important times in history. He is also in the folklore of the region known as Middle Tennessee. I first heard about Bob in my youth. I came across him again when I was doing research for a guided tour on the African-American heritage of Nashville. Conflicting stories led me to seek original documents where I found numerous mentions of Bob. Further searching caused a man and a story to develop in my mind. So, I decided to write this book.

Bob's nickname, "Black Bob," indicates that he was not of mixed race as is the case with most free people of color in colonial days. He was the first slave to gain his freedom in Middle Tennessee, and he was the first ex-slave to own property and to be recognized by a Tennessee court of law with equal legal standing. He was the subject of several lawsuits while still a slave, and he continued to make use of the court system after he obtained his freedom.

It is unequivocal that Bob knew Andrew and Rachel Jackson. Rachel Donelson Jackson and Bob were on the same perilous river voyage to the Cumberland Settlement. Jackson frequented *Black Bob's Tavern,* and the founding fathers of Middle Tennessee gathered in Bob's establishment where the events and politics of the day were discussed.

Modern day Tennessee is divided into three grand divisions. The divisions were settled at different times, separated by natural barriers and often, political philosophy. In the hearts and minds of Tennesseans, our state is the mountains of East Tennessee, the rolling hills of Middle Tennessee and the flat-delta of West Tennessee — separate, yet united through pride in our rich heritage and the volunteer spirit. At the time of this story, only portions of East and Middle Tennessee were under development; therefore, only Eastern and Western Tennessee existed.

As the author, I have attempted to make the connection between historical events and Bob. Was he there? How did he get there? Why was he there? What did he do? What did he think about it? Historical documents leave large gaps that permit one's mind to wander, and different people recording the same event have different viewpoints. As far as possible, I have remained true to history; however, when historical accounts were in conflict, I chose the version that most suited my purpose. There may be leaps of logic. I am not a historian; I simply have a story to tell of a truly remarkable man on America's colonial frontier.

Additionally, much of this period in Tennessee history involved Andrew Jackson. This story is not intended to be about Jackson; it is intended to be about Bob Renfro. It is impossible, however, to write about this time without assigning a large role to Jackson. Jackson's dominance of the period may account for why Bob has been overlooked for two hundred years.

Names are very difficult. Seldom does one find the given name of a woman, a child, or a slave in documents of this time. They are referred to only through the male patriarch's name. Unless that person is named in a legal document or achieved later fame, his/her name is lost to history. Relationships are often not available. Men with the same surname may be father and son, brothers, or any other combination of male relatives. Two or three men with an identical name are not uncommon. Spelling is another adventure in problem-solving. Even within an official court document, a name may be spelled differently. The spelling of Renfro appears as Rentfroe, Rentfro, Renfrow and Renfroe. Using the given name with the surname usually aids in making the connection. I chose one spelling and stuck with it, except in direct quotes. Another liberty I took is that in old documents and newspaper print a letter very similar to "f" represented the letter "s." I chose the modern usage. Additionally, the terms black, negro, and African were used interchangeably in official records and so, too, in this story.

Most of my characters' names are historically correct; however, it is often necessary to create a character for plot development. I trust that my family and friends will not be overly disappointed in the characters named in their honor.

ONE
PARADISE DISCOVERED – 1779

"Captain Robertson has returned!"

This news rang throughout Fort Patrick Henry on the Holston River in the summer of 1779. James Robertson had been on a trip to the Western Lands of North Carolina to determine if the area was suitable for settlement. He had explored the land along the Cumberland River at the French Lick, and his initial reports exceeded the most optimistic expectations: "It is the most beautiful and peaceful place I have ever laid my eyes on. You would not believe the amount of game — large herds of buffalo, deer, and elk. Plenty of bears and beavers. You practically have to kick rabbits and turkey out of your way. It is as close to the Promised Land as ever I hope to see," Robertson proclaimed, adding, "I have not seen a hostile in three months. I left a small party of men there to tend the corn crop we planted."

James Robertson, a Virginian by birth, stood six-feet tall with dark hair, blue eyes, and fair complexion. He had moved steadily westward in search of land and fortune. Now he was thirty-eight years old and an acknowledged leader on the frontier. Richard Henderson of the Transylvania Land Company had persuaded Robertson to explore the area that Henderson had recently purchased from a Cherokee Indian Tribe. His reward would be in land.

1

Henderson also had formed an association with sixty-two-year-old John Donelson, a wealthy man by anyone's standards who had been a member of the House of Burgesses in the Virginia Colony. He had surveyed much of Virginia's western lands and had been in numerous campaigns against the Cherokee Tribes. He had holdings in Virginia and Kentucky, but he wanted more. The thought of unlimited land wealth was too much of a lure for him to resist.

Joseph Renfro chatted briefly about Robertson's report with his brothers Moses and James before going off to find his wife, Olive. Joseph, whose hair had started to gray at the temples, had just turned forty years of age. All of the Renfros were several inches short of being six-feet tall, and with the exception of Moses, were of slim build. Olive Renfro was two years younger than her husband and still retained her youthful figure, a fact that pleased Joseph. The Renfros were part of the continuing migration from Virginia and North Carolina in search of land.

"My dear, I have just talked with Captain Robertson. His report of the Cumberland Lands is beyond belief. I'm certain Moses and Elizabeth will be moving on. I think James will too. I'm not sure about brother Isaac and Lucille. Uncle Peter and Aunt Mary will wait."

"And you think we should move on too?"

"The land is plentiful and cheap. Richard Henderson is the land agent, and he says the Transylvania Company will sell thousand-acre plots. The first to go will not have to pay until the crops come in. The land here is not that good for farming. Too many hills."

"What about the war? We came here not only for land, but also to fight the war."

"We've done our best to win independence from the British. We have fought the Cherokee until they are no longer a threat around here. Captain Witcher says that Colonel Shelby is preparing his militia regiment to move on the Chickamauga Cherokee towns down river. We do not know what is happening in the other colonies. By moving west, we can claim that land and make it free."

Olive Renfro began to reminisce. When she married Joseph, she thought they were just moving a little westward in Virginia. Now they were in the region of North Carolina, just south of the Virginia border that was considered the frontier. She had not been prepared for frontier life, but she had learned. And now that they seemed to be safe, her husband wanted her to pack up their family and move. She decided she would talk with Charlotte Robertson personally before committing.

As the Renfros were concluding their conversation, three youths entered the clearing near the fort, a red hound bounding before them. Two of them were toting their hunting trophy attached to a pole resting on their shoulders. The one in front was carrying all three long rifles and was quite a sight to behold: He was of medium height and build, wore a shortened version of a hunting shirt made of deerskin and deerskin leggings laced to just below the knee of his broadcloth pants. A hunting knife and a tomahawk were tucked into the belt holding his shirt together. A string of bear claws was dangling from his neck. He did not wear a hat. While his clothing and stature were most interesting, his most distinguishing feature was that he was as black as the bear hanging between his white companions.

Joseph could see him through the open gate.

"Olive, do you think that boy knows he's a slave?"

"Of course. Bob knows he's our property. Why do you ask such a foolish question?"

"Well, he comes and goes as he pleases. Why, he goes out hunting almost everyday."

"And whose larder has more bear grease in it than any other? And who sets the best table in this fort. And dear Joseph, might I remind you, just who gave him that rifle?"

"It's just that since your father made you a present of him…."

"When Father gave him to us after my brother Frank died, Bob was just a child—not as old as our own son. He needed more caring for than he could help out. But, then we started moving west. He learned to track and to fight Indians before he even learned to plant crops. We don't have a house for him to learn to be a houseboy, but still, he helps out and does any chore either of us gives him. I never want for firewood or water. Besides, he has such a cheerful disposition, you can't help but laugh at him."

"Look at him now; he looks more like an Indian than some Indians I've seen."

"True, but I do believe he shot the deer, skinned it, tanned the hide, and stitched the shirt and boots. I recall that we ate the deer. And if my memory serves me, that hunting shirt you are so fond of…"

"I surrender. You win, my dearest."

The youths entered the fort and walked toward the Renfros. Bob had his usual infectious smile.

"Good day Master Renfro, Mistress Renfro; we eat good dis night."

"And just why are they doing the heavy toting?" Joseph asked, containing his smile behind a stern face.

"'Cause I kilt the bear. That be fair, don't ya think?"

"We'll talk about that some other time. You better get that animal skinned if you don't want the meat to spoil. I suppose the hide is yours too?"

Bob only grinned wider. "Yes, suh. They gets half the meat and the claws. I already got 'nough claws."

Several things set Bob apart from the Renfros. He did not sit down at the same table; he did not sleep in the same room, and he was not being taught to read the Bible and copy the words on a slate. None of this disturbed him though; he had never been a part of it, so he did not miss it. He knew there was a difference, but it seemed natural to him. He slept in a little lean-to at the rear of the Renfro cabin. Late at night, when the settlement was asleep, he often visited with the other slaves. Many of them were recent purchases of Captain Donelson. Occasionally, someone would talk about the poor treatment of slaves on some of the old plantations, but none of them had been beaten. For the most part they worked side-by-side with their masters. The men told Bob he was property, just the same as a horse was property. He did not understand this concept. To his way of thinking, he belonged *with*, not *to*, the Renfros, and if he was like a horse, he was the top horse in the stable. Still, nobody wanted to be a slave.

Patsy, the cook of the Donelson family, often fed Bob in return for what he added to the pot. It was a source of amusement to both of them that when the often-pompous Captain Donelson put his feet under the table to enjoy a hearty meal, it was due to two Africans. Patsy liked to talk about how things were back in Virginny where she had the proper equipment for cooking. "Ain't much good-tasting food cooked fast. You gots to prepare and season. It takes time and just the right 'mount of heat. Even cookin' on open fires, you gets the meat too close to the flame, it gets burnt and not fit to eat."

Patsy was the only African that Bob knew well or would call a friend. He knew others and liked a few of them, particularly Prometheus, a gentle giant belonging to Moses Renfro. As a rule, Prometheus didn't have much to say, but it was he who cautioned Bob that white folks didn't like it if black people spoke "too good."

"They gots to think they smarter 'n you. If'n you get uppity with yo' speech, they thinks you trying to be good as they are. It just the way things be. No reason to ask for problems," Prometheus had cautioned him.

Bob had not been around many black people. As a child he learned to talk as Olive taught her son William. He learned the essentials of communication, but his grammar was not corrected as the Renfro children's was. There was seldom an occasion to practice the art of conversation with educated people. He was a natural mimic and a fast learner. He had observed that there was a slight difference in the way Olive Renfro taught her children what she called "manners." Bob was expected to be more respectful, and over time, he had adopted words and phrases that acknowledged he knew his place. Lack of instruction had caused his everyday dialect to be similar to that of other black people in the settlement.

The following morning Olive sought out Charlotte Reeves Robertson. Mrs. Robertson was with Rachel Stockley Donelson, the wife of Captain John Donelson. They were at the well in the center of the fort.

Olive greeted them, "Good morning, ladies. The Lord has given us a beautiful day."

Rachel Donelson was the first to acknowledge the greeting. "Indeed He has."

"Joseph tells me you will be moving on soon."

"Yes we are. Surely you are going with us?"

"We haven't decided." Olive was seeking information but did not want to ask too many questions.

"My James's description is of a virtual paradise. Imagine, the Garden of Eden right here in North Carolina."

"I just don't know if I want to walk my girls that far," Olive ventured her first inquiry. "How far is it anyway?"

"As the crow flies, it's less than two hundred and fifty miles. But, Dear Lady, you won't have to walk that far. Captain Donelson has a plan."

Rachel Donelson took up the conversation: "As you may know, my husband is much experienced in the handling of boats. He says that we can get on a boat right here on the Holston River and float downstream most of the way, just relaxing and enjoying the scenery. We can be less than a hundred miles from our destination in three weeks. He has the maps, and there is more to the plan. James and John are with Richard Henderson as we speak, working out the details. It is sure to be a great adventure!"

"Still, I just don't know. I don't think the Lord meant for me to live the pioneer life."

"Look at it this way," Charlotte encouraged, "James and I already have a large family and no doubt there will be more. We can never accumulate an inheritance for our sons or a dowry for our daughters here. Along the Cumberland, wealth is there for the taking. We will put plow to the ground, plant the seeds, and it will spring forth."

Olive was not yet convinced. "It all sounds too good to be true. Then, the Lord does work in mysterious ways."

"Yes, dear, and remember — He helps those most who help themselves."

"Amen," was the choral-like response.

II

Joseph Renfro attended every meeting as James Robertson and John Donelson put forth their plan; Robertson would lead a party of men and older boys. They would drive everyone's livestock overland. Driving cattle, sheep, and swine would be slow; it might take more than a month. They could live off of the land. Once there, they would start the construction of a stockade and cabins. Captain Donelson would wait a month before he started the downstream journey. The Holston River flows south and is joined by the French Broad River and several minor streams to form the Tennessee River. It is then joined by the Clinch River and continues to flow south to the border with the Georgia Colony, and then it turns westward. They would meet on the river due south of the proposed Cumberland settlement. The rendezvous point was unmistakable — a place called Muscle Shoals in the Mississippi Territory. There the river was extremely dangerous; the roar of the rushing water could be heard for miles. Robertson would bring pack animals to carry the farm tools and household goods they were to bring. They would arrive at their new home in another week, a total of one month from beginning to end. All would be in place for spring planting. What could be better?

The Renfro families met to talk things over. Moses, the eldest, was the acknowledged leader. Isaac was the more cautious of the brothers.

"I have decided we are going. I've looked over the maps, and I know exactly where I want to claim land," Moses declared.

"How can you know, sight unseen?" challenged an irritated Isaac.

"I've talked to trappers who have seen it. There is a little river called the Red less than fifty miles to the northwest of where Robertson is settling. It empties into the Cumberland. Between us, we would control several thousand acres along both sides of our own river, and it is just a short way from Captain Robertson's settlement."

"How many boats will we need?" asked James, his mind made up.

"I figure three mid-sized boats with a shelter on them and a couple of canoes tied behind. Captain Donelson is talking about one big boat for his family. He will transport Captain Robertson's family and Robertson's sister, the Widow Johnston, and her children. He'll have his sons to help. Along with their negroes, he can control a big boat. We don't have his experience, so I would rather use smaller boats. Maybe two families on each boat."

"Don't count me in just yet," Joseph cautioned. "We are still thinking and praying over this matter."

"The same goes for us," added Isaac.

Isaac called Joseph aside for a private meeting.

"Which way you leaning, Isaac?"

"To be truthful, I'm not keen on a water journey. Too much can go wrong. I'm not so sure John Donelson is the riverman he claims to be. But, I do lean toward getting my share of all that free land. What about you?"

"If I go, it'll be by water. Olive is reluctant. She wants William to go back to Virginia to be properly educated and be a gentleman. You know how she is about him. He's almost twenty-one, but she is still protective of him. I know she has no intention of walking two hundred and fifty miles. If it was by wagon, maybe. But it's all wilderness, so wagons are out of the question. The only persuasion I can use on that Bible-reading woman is that we will be carrying the Word of God westward."

After a bit of thought Joseph added, "We've got plenty of time before Captain Donelson leaves. The problem is that everyone will need a boat. If we are going, we need to make arrangements to have our boats built."

"What do you think it will cost?"

"Doesn't make much difference, I'll have to barter my part."

"What about your negro?"

"Bob? You mean barter him? He rightfully belongs to Olive. Her father gave him to us when her little brother died. No, Bob goes where we go. Besides, he is a better hunter than I."

Olive Renfro at last gave her nod of approval. She told her family that this was for them. Not only would they spread "The Word," but they would also find their futures and their fortunes in the new land.

Bob accompanied Joseph to see the man who would direct the building of boats, Francis Hodgson. He was a weather-beaten little man and known to have a bad disposition when things didn't go his way. He was not in a good mood this day.

"I'll be hard pressed to fill the orders I've already got," Hodgson scolded Joseph. "You should have come sooner."

It was not just the lumber; it was the manpower too. Captain Donelson's big boat was going to take most of his time, and Captain Blackmore wanted boats built and delivered to him on the Clinch River.

"I need more men. Fieldhands don't make good boat builders. It takes a different kind of skill. Captain Donelson is sending some of his hands, but it'll take all of them to build the boats he wants."

"I wanted to talk to you about that too. What if I and my boy here hire on with you to help cover the cost?"

"We might work something out. Your boy don't look all that strong. But that's your problem. I'll tell you what, you cut the timber, then peel it, and help cut it into boards. You get enough for five boats, help with the construction, and one of them will be yours. I'll show you the trees to cut."

"Done."

"One more thing," Hodgson injected. "You help me pole the boats up to Captain Donelson and to Captain Blackmore down on the Clinch. It'll be good training for you on handling a boat."

"Agreed."

The trees Hodgson selected were called tulip poplar. Its name came from the beautiful tulip-like, green-orange bloom that appeared on the tree in late spring. The tree grew tall and straight. Some reached almost two-hundred feet into the air, frequently, showing 50-100 feet of trunk without a branch. The width and length of boards could be whatever the builder wanted. The wood was rot and insect-resistant. Smaller trees were ideal for constructing log cabins.

Within days, Joseph and Bob were sore and aching, but uncomplaining. They were on a mission. Olive insisted that William, or Billy as she still called him, stay with her. Joseph talked to Bob about what it would be like in the new land.

"Ever'body taking their blacks?" asked Bob.

"Of course. They will be needed to help clear the land and plant the seeds."

"Not much gonna change for them then."

"Maybe not, but at our place we'll have a fine new house someday, and you'll have your own place out back. Won't be too long you'll be asking us to find you a wife."

Bob's mouth went silent. His mind became even more active. He had given this subject consideration before. "Wife! What would I want with a wife? If'n she had chill'uns, and they all do, they would be the property of whoever owned her. No thank you, suh. My chill'uns ain't gonna be some white man's fieldhands."

After a brief silence, Bob asked, "Your brothers got a boat too?"

"They are making their own arrangements. Isaac is not ready to leave else he would be helping us. Moses let Mister Hodgson use his big man Prometheus. Master Moses will trade everything but his own labor. The axe handle has not been made that fits my big brother's hand. James will do what Moses says."

They chuckled at the humor. Both realized they had shared a confidence not to be repeated in front of others. Joking about one's white brother with a black man was not done. Their teamwork, for just a moment in time, had transcended the gulf between master and slave.

III

The leaves had turned early in the fall of 1779. All the crops were harvested. Frost was on the ground every morning. By mid-November, Captain Robertson gathered his party. It seemed that all the boys and young men over fifteen, some even younger, were going on the overland journey, with the exception of the Donelsons and Billy Renfro. The gathering of animals was a disorganized and humorous mess. It hadn't been intended that way, but the inexperienced boys drove all the animals into one large herd. Boys wrestled pigs and sheep trying to move the unwilling animals where they wanted them. Robertson's ten-year-old son Jonathan was having trouble with a big ram that had been assigned to his care. Holding a herd of mixed animals together was abandoned, so there were separate herds for cattle, sheep, and swine. A few men were mounted on horses. More horses, donkeys, and mules would be herded. Others were to be used as pack animals. Twelve hounds trained to the horn were lying about waiting for the command. Men and boys said good-bye to their wives and mothers. For some of the boys, it was the first time to be separated from their mothers. Their partings were awkward, but they were off to prove their fitness for manhood. William looked on, wishing to leave with them but not wanting to confront his mother.

Captain Robertson would follow a route that Daniel Boone had recommended. Boone was a well-known trailblazer from Pennsylvania. Richard Henderson and Boone were also partners in a similar venture for the settlement of Kentucky. Robertson had used the same route in his exploration journey, and knew it to be safe with a minimum of difficulty. He would go northwest, then westward across Kentucky before turning south to the French Salt Lick. Once there, he would build the fort on the bluffs overlooking the river.

Joseph and Bob watched them leave before they went into the woods. They had become a precision team. Both had become muscular. Bob would soon need a new shirt, though he usually worked without it once the sun was high.

"Master Renfro, when we gonna do all the other things that gots to be done befo' we leave?"

"We've almost filled our contract. Our boat is coming along. We've got a good supply of smoked and dried meat, but maybe a couple of bears would be good. We'll go hunting. I've noticed bears are getting hard to find in these parts. The wife and girls are drying beans and fruits. We'll have potatoes and turnips too. Some household goods are being packed in barrels. Keeping everything dry is important. The journey is not long."

"Yes, suh. Why we travelin' in win'er? That don't seem like a good idea to me."

"I think the idea is we'll be going south. They say it's warmer in the South."

"Rufus say then we goin' back no'th once we start walkin'."

"We are. We just have to trust Captain Robertson and Captain Donelson."

15

"Yes, suh, I guess we do. But even so, no matter where we be, win'er is a comin' on. Is it all right to make coats for the mistress and your little uns?"

"Well sure, if you have time. Just what do you intend to make the coats out of?"

"I got that bear and a few more hides."

"You have enough for three coats? Where did you get them?"

"I got plenty. Some I fixed myself; others I did me a little swappin' on."

"Bob, I do believe you have the makings of a natural-born trader."

As the flatboats were finished, they had to be delivered. Fort Patrick Henry was about half a mile upstream from the yard where the boats were being constructed. As his final test, Mister Hodgson would stroll around on the boat checking it out, as Billy manned the tiller, and Joseph and Bob poled the craft. Hodgson warned, "Nothing to it when it's empty. It'll be different when she has a load on her."

Captain Donelson took delivery of his boat. It took more than three men to get it upstream. Delivering boats to Captain Blackmore on the Clinch River was a pleasure. They all took turns handling the boat in the downstream currents and as lookouts keeping the boat off rocks and shoals. After poling the boat upstream on the Clinch, they would go hunting on their way back. Billy reveled in these trips. Away from the watchful eye of his mother, he was doing what every young man should be doing on the frontier. Being sickly as a baby and having a fever when he was twelve had made him small, but not as fragile as his mother thought. Joseph, for the first time, was enjoying his son's company.

The end of November found the lumber contract finished. The Joseph Renfro family took great pride in their new boat. Billy had assisted them in its construction. The workmanship was the finest. Joseph and Mister Hodgson had discussed and agreed on some design changes from the flatboats Captain Donelson insisted on. Hodgson had some ideas that he wanted to try out: "I know flatboats will do for what Captain Donelson wants, but all they do is float. If you want a real boat, it should look more like sea-going ships. We can make one with a shallow draft. Besides, flatboats are ugly. A man needs to feel he created something good. This boat will carry sail if you need it."

When finished, the boat sat about three feet out of the water with a slight angle on the hull but with a flat bottom for negotiating shallow water. It came to a sharp point at the bow and measured thirty-two feet long and nine feet wide. Its cabin was twelve by five. Goods could be stored forward and aft of the cabin with room to maneuver around its deck. They would tow a small skiff.

As the Renfro family assembled to view their new boat, Bob was holding the hand of the youngest, Sarah, to keep her from getting too close to the water, while Joseph completed his assessment. "We should name our boat. Captain Donelson calls his *Adventure*."

"How about, *Papa's Folly,* from what Mother says…"

"You shut up, Billy. It should be, *Papa's Dream*," his offended sister responded.

"Susan is right; it is my dream. But we are seeking paradise. I suggest *Paradise Seeker*."

"According to everyone here we are bound for paradise," Olive added in a dry tone.

Olive Renfro had the last word. They started to accumulate the provisions to be put aboard the *Paradise Bound*.

TWO
THE JOURNEY BEGINS – 1779

Late November and early December were occupied with the accumulation process. Families were gathering the supplies and foods they thought would be most needed for the journey, as well as during the first few weeks in the Cumberland Settlement. By common consent it was agreed that every family was on its own. They would travel together; however, food and shelter were the responsibility of each individual family. Olive Renfro was a cautious woman and commanded, "We will take everything our boat will hold. We can discard it later, or perhaps trade for something we do need."

Most of the extra load was food. Joseph and Bob had hunted almost every day. They dried and smoked most of the deer and bear meat. Bear fat had been rendered and stored away. They participated in a "hog killing" during the first cold snap. Working on shares, they had accumulated a pork ham, smoked side meat, and some salted pork. After viewing Bob's treasure-trove of hides and furs, Joseph decided they didn't need more, so new hides were traded for powder and gunshot. Olive and the girls tapped maple trees and boiled the sap, producing sugar and thick syrups. Agreements were made with friends and neighbors for joint ventures in the production of vegetables and fruits.

In the early morning hours of December 22, 1779, the first day of winter, the Donelson Party gathered by the light of the nearly full moon. About thirty families were making the journey — forty men and one hundred and twenty women and children. Some thirty slaves were to accompany their masters on this Exodus to the Promised Land. The Renfros, Moses, James, and Joseph had three men per boat, including slaves. Nathan and Solomon Turpin, relatives of the Renfros, had joined the group. With the women and growing boys, they felt they had the manpower to handle any situation. Olive Renfro, dressed in a full-length bearskin coat, was still uneasy. She gazed at her young family. Susan and Sarah were dressed in their new bearskin coats trimmed with a white fur and white hats; Joseph and Billy had robes of buffalo hides draped about their shoulders, as did Bob. All of the males had new hunting shirts and two pairs of leggings to cover their feet up to their knees. One must keep their leggings dry, as wet feet were considered to be the cause of rheumatism.

The *Adventure* was by far the largest craft. About 65-feet long, its shape was a rectangle that sloped upward in both the front and the back. Captain Donelson stood on top of the cabin holding the tiller. The boat was steered by a rudder attached to a long tiller pole that lay through a y-shaped yoke about five feet above the rear deck. In addition to his large family, Captain Donelson, was transporting Charlotte Robertson and her children, along with her twenty-two-year-old widowed sister-in-law Ann Robertson Johnston and her three little girls. More than thirty people were on board. A second Donelson boat carried more possessions and slaves. John Donelson, Jr., manned its tiller. *Paradise Bound* stood out because of some of the

20

innovations incorporated into her design. Joseph Renfro stood on the deck to handle his much shorter tiller. He felt some hostility, or perhaps envy, toward the sleeker looking craft. Some felt it was unnecessarily pretentious. Olive Renfro, normally a prudent woman favoring plain things, approved of the *Paradise Bound* design. It was safer for her family and less troublesome for her husband to steer.

Several families' boats were little more than crude rafts of logs lashed together. They had few possessions and were trusting in the Lord and the land of plenty to provide them with the substances of life. Most had some type of structure on board for protection from the weather and possibly to provide sleeping quarters when conditions did not permit sleeping on shore. A few families and men accompanying the party manned canoes of various sizes. They had their possessions bundled in oiled cloth and stowed in their canoes. Apparently, most intended to live off of the land as they traveled. Among them was a free man of color, Jack Civil.

Jack Civil was the son of a white father and a black mother. He was a free man of about twenty-five years of age. It was his hope that he would have opportunity in the new land. He had the financial resources to purchase land. Richard Henderson had assured him that his condition of birth would make no difference when it came to purchasing tracts of land.

After a prayer asking Almighty God's blessing and protection on their trip, the company was ready to begin their journey into history. Big Prometheus placed his pole into the water and on command pushed off Moses Renfro's boat. Others fell in line. They were traveling downstream in high spirits and at a leisurely pace. John Donelson had opened a book containing blank pages and entered, "Journal of a Voyage, intended by God's Permission, in the good Boat Adventure, from Fort Patrick Henry on Holston river to the French Salt-Springs on Cumberland river, kept by John Donelson." For the next eight weeks he was to have little to enter in his journal. Less than a half-mile down stream, *Adventure* ran aground on the shoal at Reedy Creek. Before a successful effort could be made to free it, winter set in. It was a winter the likes of which none of them had ever witnessed. Ice formed in the river. A rider went from the fort to tell Captain Blackmore of the delay. For nearly six weeks, the *Adventure* was stuck at the spot where Colonel Daniel Boone had started construction of the Wilderness Road only five years before. The water finally rose, and they broke loose. The freezing weather had been hard on the boats. They tied up near where Francis Hodgson had overseen their construction for the repairs. Two weeks, and a half-mile later, they were stuck again on the shoal at Poor Valley. After unloading about thirty passengers, the *Adventure* was free and floating in deep water. Olive was more than disturbed as she voiced her concerns to her husband.

"We have already consumed as much of our provisions as we expected to use in the entire journey, and we've not even got a good start. The weather has been too frightful for hunting parties to have much success; what are we to do, Joseph?"

"We follow Captain Donelson. Our choice has been made. There is nothing behind us. We must go on. Bob and I can keep us in food. We are far better off than most of these poor wretches. No one has deserted this party. We all know our future lies ahead of us."

"I am not so concerned about meat. Our potatoes, corn, beans, squash, and dried fruit are about half of what we started with. We will just have to make do with less."

When they reached the mouth of the Clinch, Captain Blackmore and his party of six boats joined them. The little fleet began to make the type of progress they had expected when the journey was planned, but not without incident. They lost the first member of their party when Ruben Harrison went out hunting and did not return. Thomas Hutchingson's slave died after his feet and legs were frozen. While camped at an abandoned Chickamauga town, a baby was born to the wife of Ephraim Peyton, a man who had gone overland with Captain Robertson.

They felt secure knowing that Colonel Shelby had recently defeated and made peace with the tribes of this region. But the next three days brought disaster. Indians began attacks and one young man was killed. Following an outbreak of smallpox, twenty-eight members of the party were isolated. By common agreement, they lagged behind the main party. They were also attacked and killed by Indians. Next the survivors encountered the whirlpool called the Big Suck. Believing the bigger boats offered the greatest security, John Cotton's family had taken refuge on Robert Cartwright's boat. Cotton's canoe, which was attached to the Cartwright boat, overturned. They had stopped in an attempt to retrieve the cargo when Indians appeared on the bluffs above and began firing. Due to its shallow draft, *Paradise Bound* was able to move in between *Adventure* and the shore. Bob grabbed his rifle, leaped on to *Adventure*, and began to return fire. A girl moved next to him in an attempt to help. "You just in my way, girl. You gonna get us both kilt. Get behind cover and stay down!" Bob spoke forcefully, and she moved away. As *Adventure* and *Paradise Bound* moved away, they saw the Jennings family boat hit the rocks. A negro man and a young white man went into the water. Mrs. Jennings, her nearly grown son, a negro woman, and Mrs. Peyton were desperately trying to save the boat as Mr. Jennings fired at the Indians.

Two days later the Jennings boat reappeared, badly damaged and without its cargo. The Peyton baby had been killed in the confusion. The men who went into the water were missing, and the survivors were distributed among other boats. They had to keep moving until nightfall.

The following morning, Sunday, March 12, they shoved off while it was still dark, under a new moon not yet in its first quarter. After a few hours they encountered another Indian town. They were fired upon and returned fire as they passed. Two hours later they heard the roar of Muscle Shoals and spotted the rendezvous point. At long last, their ordeal would be over. Their salvation was on shore in the person of James Robertson.

THREE
THE RESCUE - 1780

John Donelson approached Moses and Joseph Renfro. Donelson didn't look much like a leader of men. His clothes had become tattered and caked with mud from scouting the riverbank, but he still maintained a look of determination. The entire party had become bedraggled. The wild Tennessee River, hostile Indians, miserable weather, and muddy riverbanks had all conspired to alter their appearance from those hearty souls on a pleasant boat ride in search of the Cumberland Settlement to one of desperate survivors.

Moses looked up as John approached. His beard had grown long. Briars and huckleberries had snagged it during the search for James Robertson's sign.

"Captain Donelson?"

"How should we proceed, gentlemen, by river or by foot?"

"Not much of a choice. What are our chances?"

"We can start walking north, or we can stay on the river. The map shows the river will turn north. We'll still be floating. When we get to the mouth, some two hundred miles from here, we have to go up stream a good twenty-five miles, find the Cumberland, and go upstream again close to another two hundred miles. All of our planning, including the size of my boat, was based on floating downstream. The question is, 'Is it better to pole these craft upstream, or walk hoping to find the proper trail and fight off hostile Indians?'"

Joseph, looking at his small family, added his thoughts, "If we walk, we have to leave most of our equipment behind. Captain Robertson was to have horses, mules, and additional men here. Pack animals cannot be replaced by women and children."

"True. However, we don't know how perilous the waters are. We are stopped here because we know the next thirty miles are dangerous — fast flowing water with rocks in the stream. I think my crew can handle the *Adventure*. Canoes and small craft will make it. There are six or seven hours of daylight left. We should go now before anyone has time to become frightened. Can you make it?"

"Lead the way."

They gathered the entire party and went over the options. The roaring water provided a somber background. Most looked on in astonished bewilderment. Finally, the young widow, Ann Robertson Johnston, broke the silence, "We have not come this far and endured as we have to give up here. As for my children and myself, we are prepared to put our faith in the Lord and Captain Donelson. He knows how to travel the river."

Charlotte Robertson expressed her deepest thoughts, "I fear something has happened to James. If it were humanly possible, he would have been here. I don't know where we are headed or what dangers lie ahead. One thing is certain, we cannot go back. We know certain death is behind us. The last thing my husband said to me was, 'follow Captain

Donelson; no matter what happens, go where he leads,' and that is what me and mine will do."

"Amen" came from somewhere in the crowd, followed by a chorus of "Amen."

"So be it," affirmed John Donelson. "Make sure everything is tied down and secure. Johnny, you make certain that we have sturdy poles on every boat. We can't have them breaking in this stretch or we'll flounder on the rocks."

John Donelson, Jr., understood and set to his task while his bride Mary looked on. It briefly crossed her mind that this was more than she had bargained for; this was to be her honeymoon trip. Then she looked around at her female companions and their children. "I wonder if it was like this when Moses led the children of Israel. If he had a few women like these, it wouldn't have taken him forty years." She determined that she would follow their example. There would not be another complaint from her.

While the meeting was going on, Bob huddled with the other slaves. "We be dead men fo' sure," voiced Rufus. "I say we take-off into the woods."

"And do what?" asked Bob. "We been a part of killin' them redskins. You think they gonna welcome us? If they followin', they likely to kill us. I ain't ever had no problem with Master Renfro. He treats me good. I go where he goes. I ain't tryin' to stop you. You do what you wants, all of you."

Jack Civil approached the group. "This ain't the time boys. I know what you's thinking. This ain't the time. You all be dead 'fore the next sunrise — if not from redskins or wild beasts, your own masters will hunt you down. This ain't the time."

"Ain't nobody talkin' 'bout runnin' away," Rufus was emphatic. "We just talkin' 'bout how best to get on with it."

The last minute preparations were made. The disheveled party gathered for a final prayer. Captain Donelson was a flurry of activity, issuing orders and directing actions. "Jack you lead off in your canoe. Pick a direct route. We can't swing these boats much. Be cautious, but go slow enough that we can see you. You will be marking the way. Pick passages big enough for these boats to follow through. Two more canoes follow him, then my boat. Put a canoe in front of each boat. Moses, would you be the last boat?"

"It would be my honor."

"All right," he commanded. "Shove off!"

Every woman said her silent prayer. All of *Paradise Bound*'s passengers heard a feminine voice intone, "God be with us." Chance placed their boat second in line. They were ready and moved off, keeping *Adventure* in sight, with a canoe between them.

Bob moved to his place on the right front. His job was to keep the boat off the rocks on that side. William was on the other side. The boat moved into the current and picked up speed. Part of *Adventure* disappeared between the swells. The roar of the water was deafening. The boat pitched and dipped as the water rose and fell. At times the canoe between the two boats completely disappeared. By now, Joseph Renfo was an expert with the tiller. He maneuvered his boat with ease in the early going. Bob was enjoying the ride. The speed was exhilarating. Then he saw what was ahead! The big rocks loomed.

On *Adventure*, size was creating problems. It did not respond to the tiller as well as it had in the slow moving current. It took all of Captain Donelson's skill just to keep the bow headed forward. Thus far, the men on the sides were able to keep it from the rocks. Teamwork quickly developed. Extra men, black and white, rushed into position whenever they saw the boat was approaching a rock because one man could not push the massive boat off on a direct approach. The idea was to hit a glancing blow and recover until they approached the next rock. Young Rachel could not contain her curiosity. She crept from the safe place her father had told her to stay for a better view. She stood up just as the boat approached a dangerous rock. Four men stabbed at the rock. It jolted the boat, staggered the girl, and she flipped headlong into the water.

Bob saw the girl fall. He knew immediately it was the same girl he had cautioned earlier to get out of his way before she got them both killed. He motioned to his master and pointed. Joseph Renfro nodded and made a slight adjustment with his tiller. He assumed Bob saw something in the water and was pointing out a safer route. The canoe apparently did not see her at all. They were on the left side, and *Adventure* blocked their view. The girl bobbed up, coughing and spitting. She was amazingly calm. She bobbed some more and raised her arm into the air. Bob thought, "She thinks she can float out of this. This water is too cold. She catch her death if'n she don't drown." She was drifting toward a rock and so was the Renfro boat. Bob positioned his pole to take on the rock. "We gonna crush her if'n I miss." His pole struck the rock, and the boat shifted to the left as he reached for the out-stretched hand. In one motion, he snatched the child from the water and drew her onto the boat. She hit the deck and rolled to the feet of an astonished Olive Renfro. Bob's hand returned to grip the pole, ready for the next rock.

One hour later the boats came to calm water and were rendezvousing with the *Adventure* where a distraught mother was being comforted. "We have her!" shouted Joseph Renfro. Rachel moved to the front of the boat. Mrs. Renfro had stripped her of her wet clothing and wrapped her in a blanket. She and her children rubbed the shivering girl vigorously, even though all the while they were being tossed about. Rachel smiled and waved to her family as casually as returning from prayer meeting.

"But, how?" asked a perplexed John Donelson.

"The Lord works in mysterious ways," Olive Renfro concluded.

II

They made camp early that night. Bob went with Joseph Renfro to hunt. Several hunting parties returned just as darkness fell. Joseph had shot a small doe, and Bob had field dressed the animal and was on the back end of the pole the two men carried. The fire was ready. The animal was butchered and shared with those who were less fortunate in the hunt. There was plenty to go around. A man and a child approached the Renfro camp. "I can't thank you enough for saving her," a humbled John Donelson extended his hand to Joseph.

"To be truthful, John, it was my man Bob that pulled her from the water."

John Donelson could not bring himself to show gratitude to a slave, but he managed a nod in Bob's direction. Both kept their eyes downcast. He moved back to his fire. Young Rachel lagged behind to chat with Mrs. Renfro and the children. "Miss Ann says we can take a day away from our lessons. My mother says I can ride with you tomorrow if it meets with your approval."

"That would be lovely, child."

Rachel waited until she knew she would have to pass Bob to reach the Donelson fire. As she passed, she spoke softly, "Thank you, Bob; thank you for saving me."

"You most welcome, Missy. You be mo' careful next time." Bob was certain there would be a next time. This beautiful and brave child would never be cautious.

John Donelson sat by the fire thinking of how to record today's events in his journal. He decided that a slave pulling a girl from the water, even if she was his child, was not worthy of mention. This was, after all, to be a historic account. Every little detail could not be written down. One such detail not written down but noticed by Bob was that for the first time, Master Renfro referred to him as "my man" rather than "my boy."

The next morning Bob noticed that there was a difference in the way the people were behaving toward him. Throughout the night, the story of the rescue had been told and retold. By morning, most of the party was convinced they had actually witnessed it. Men pointed him out. Children spoke to him. Some of the women even smiled and nodded in his direction. "Being a man sho' be different," he thought.

But Jack Civil brought him back to reality. "Don't over do it," he said virtually spitting the bitter words out, "You still black, and you still a slave."

III

Miss Rachel Donelson was onboard *Paradise Bound* when they shoved off. The going was easy. Bob was on the tiller; Joseph sat on a keg up forward acting as the lookout. William busied himself making sure the load was still secure. Olive and the girls chatted and told stories. They all laughed as they described Rachel being plucked from the water and deposited at their feet "looking like a drowned 'possum." Still they knew how near she had come to meeting her Maker.

"I think this is a good time to read some Scripture," Olive proclaimed, "The light is so good now. It's difficult to read by the campfire, and we are always so busy."

She rummaged among her belongings and brought forth her Bible.

"Read about Uncle Moses," Sarah implored.

"He ain't our Uncle Moses. He just has the same name," her knowing sister corrected.

"I don't need to have it read to me. I know it by heart," Rachel bragged.

"It won't hurt to have it read just in case you forgot a few words," Olive admonished firmly.

Bob could hear the story being read. He was still giving thought as to why white men were given the right to own black people. And why white men were so convinced it was proper to kill red men and take their land. He had reasoned that it must have something to do with this book they were so

33

fond of reading; all of them had one. He leaned closer for better hearing. Olive took notice and spoke louder. It was her Christian duty to bring the word of the Lord to all who should hear it. It was her naïve assumption that since her family had owned Bob for as long as she could remember, he must be a Christian. Bob, in fact, didn't think much about religion one way or the other. But he did enjoy the readings. They were good stories: some with morals, some with adventure and war, and some with some powerful sinful goings-on.

As the day wore on, the Renfros fell asleep. Rachel was too energetic for sleeping during the day, so she positioned herself near Bob. "Would you like for me to tell you some more Bible stories?"

"You can tell me mo' 'bout this Moses man if'n you wants. I kind o' likes him."

"Well, he freed the children of Israel from Pharaoh."

"Master Renfro own them too?"

"Not Renfro, Pharaoh!" Rachel realized that Bob was funning her. She went on. "He was like a king. His army drowned in the Red Sea. They were chasing Moses and the children of Israel, so God helped him."

"Kind of like us?"

"Bob, why do you think that we're like them?"

"Well, we be goin' to where the land is peaceful and free. I ain't heard of no milk and honey, but there be plentiful game. We escaped on the river. You pulled from the river just like Moses when he was a baby. We be chased by redskins. We need Providence to help us. That be close enough."

"You're impossible!" Rachel could see the vague connections, or was he still just funning?

"Tell me, Miss Rachel, do God mean for all people to be free or just those Moses chill'un?"

"I don't know. There is a lot about slaves in the Bible. Maybe some people are meant to be slaves."

"Do it say people like me are to be slaves?"

"Don't know. I'll have to study on it."

They both realized they were sharing a familiarity that could not be done in front of others. It was an unwritten law, and all knew it was the law. Rachel made a decision though: "This black man saved my life. I promise before God that I will help him to become a free man." She didn't know how or when, but she would do it!

True to Captain Donelson's prediction, the river turned north. Ann Johnston resumed lessons for the children. Rachel spent more time with the Renfros. She felt a level of comfort when she was near Bob. She noticed that he took an interest in their lessons and Scripture readings.

"Would you like to read my Bible sometimes?"

"Missy, I can't read a word in it. You knows black people can't learn to read."

"That's nonsense. Everybody's been talking about how smart you are and how you remember things. I'll teach you. What Miss Ann tells us, I will tell you."

"Missy, you gonna get us both in trouble."

"It'll be our secret. We'll start with small words. Do you even know your letters?"

"I knows some numbers. Have to learn numbers to get the right amount of most everything. Master Renfro got everything with a number on it. He tell me which one to fetch, 'n I go get it."

"See, there you are; you can learn to read. You just need to learn to put letters together to make words. Putting letters together is what makes words. It's so simple."

Rachel turned learning into a game. The Renfro children became unknowing instructors. They pointed to letters painted on barrels and boxes, anything that had been labeled, and pronounced the letters and the words. The parents were so proud of their scholarly pursuits that they too joined in. Most of this was done within earshot of Bob. Sometimes at night Rachel would take a sharp stick and scratch small words in the dirt. Bob began to get the idea. Billy, aware of the little game, considered it child's play and elected to ignore it.

Captain Donelson commented to his wife that Rachel was spending too much time away from their campsite, but she defended her daughter: "It's just a phase. She feels so safe with the Renfros since they pulled her from the river. Besides, she is not neglecting her chores, and she is studying her Bible." Captain Donelson conceded—and if it didn't bother the Donelsons, it was of no concern to anyone else in the party.

One evening, Olive decided she should return the visits. She was sitting and chatting with Mrs. Donelson when the much discussed subject of Rachel's rescue came up. "We are indeed indebted to your family and your man too."

"Bob's a good man. There is very little he can't do. And he does it all without complaining. I can't remember a time Joseph had to get after him for something serious. He is as trustworthy as they come. He has had his own hunting rifle for a long time. We should find some way to reward him for what he did for young Rachel, but out here in the wilderness, what's a body to do?"

"I'll tell you what I would do if he was mine," interrupted Rachel. "A slave who saves someone's life, should get his freedom as a reward; I think that's in the Bible."

"Hush, child, I think you'll find that he must save his master's life," her mother corrected making an effort to avoid embarrassment to her guest.

Olive rose to leave, "Who knows? Maybe someday. The Lord works in mysterious ways."

IV

The days passed by quietly and slowly. There started to be a shortage of food. More and more time was consumed hunting, and the diet was becoming all meat. For the boys it was a wonderful time. They had been prevented from accompanying Captain Robertson on the overland journey because they were deemed to be too young. Now they were learning to hunt and fish. They were becoming proficient at tracking animals and setting snares. Some of the girls even became experts at catching fish. Bob told Rachel how he had seen Indians weave baskets and put them in streams. He also told her that he had seen them spear fish. This was more to her liking. A stick just the right size with a fork of strong prongs close together was selected and sharpened to a barbed point. Camp was always near a stream, and while Rachel was cautioned not to leave sight of camp, she stretched it to the limit stalking and spearing fish.

Rachel was also maturing. Bob knew he wasn't supposed to notice, but it was unavoidable. Not only was she developing into a woman, but she was also going to have stunning good looks. As he observed her standing poised over a stream with her spear looking like a young goddess, he thought, "It be a good thing they sent the young bucks with Cap'n Robertson 'cause Miss Rachel sho' would stir their blood up. That child gonna cause some po' man a lot of trouble."

On the eighth day after running the rapids at Muscle Shoals, the travelers reached the mouth of the Tennessee River. Here they faced a new river, the Ohio. It was swollen beyond its banks with run-off from snowmelts and rain. They looked at it in disbelief. How could they even consider going upstream? Several members of the party decided they had either reached their preordained destination or the limits of their endurance. They would rather take their chances in Illinois. Others planned to continue floating downstream on the Ohio to the Mississippi, where they could continue downstream eventually to Natchez and Louisiana. John Donelson made little effort to dissuade them, even though those leaving included his oldest daughter Mary and her husband John Caffery. He knew he might never see her again, but he had led this band out of the Cumberland Mountains in pursuit of a beautiful and peaceful haven on the banks of the Cumberland River, and he meant to keep that promise.

Early on the following day, the remainder of the Donelson party started upstream hoping to find the Cumberland River. They consolidated their manpower. Most of those traveling in canoes boarded *Adventure*. The Widow Johnston insisted on taking the tiller, as thirty slave and freemen poled the craft laboriously forward. *Paradise Bound* again proved to be a worthy craft. A Renfro kinsman, Nathan Turpin, joined them. Bob and Joseph, by now accustomed to teamwork, were able to keep the boat moving, but the extra pair of hands were welcomed. Billy and Olive took turns between the tiller and poling. Prometheus, Solomon Turpin and one of the families that had been traveling by canoe were persuaded to make up Moses's crew. James's crew was more difficult. He had the help of his slave, but he had to bargain for additional help. Progress was slow and painful for crews who were at their physical limits and suffering from hunger. Movement up the river was so slow that hunting parties went ashore and managed to keep up with the boats. It took eight days to reach the mouth of a river Captain Donelson believed to be the Cumberland. They left the Ohio and started upstream. The new river was more gentle and the going easier; however, they were still fatigued from the ordeal, and they were hungry.

The Donelson family had the good fortune to capture a swan floating by. It was tasty but not much when divided among such a large family. Later, they found some buffalo. The taking of a buffalo was relatively simple, but the meat did not have a good taste. Patsy told Bob it could be made better with seasoning and a little time. She then spotted a patch of green leaves that she avowed were good to eat, and she knew just how to fix them. Patsy soon had the women washing the leaves and slicing them into narrow strips. Kettles of water were brought to a boil. She approached Bob, "Now don't you hold out on me, boy. We need some fat to make these greens taste right. You got some?"

"I'll ask my mistress."

Bob approached Olive Renfro and repeated what Patsy had told him. Olive went into her stores and produced several small pieces of smoked pork and some bear fat. Buffalo was the main dish, but on that night, under Patsy's supervision, they enjoyed their fill of the greens. Captain Donelson named the greens "Shawnee Salad" in his journal, assuming that the land belonged to the Shawnee Indian Tribe. To Bob it would always be "Miss Patsy's Salad."

V

The journey resumed up the river they prayed was the Cumberland. The river was gentle so they made good progress; they had not been attacked for almost a week. The larger *Adventure* brought up the rear. Suddenly, they heard a hail from behind.

"Ahoy, John Donelson!"

It was Richard Henderson. Joy reigned. Henderson was returning from Kentucky where he had made arrangements for corn to be shipped to the Cumberland Settlement. It was their first confirmation that James Robertson was at the Cumberland and building a settlement in anticipation of their arrival. No explanation was given, nor was one asked, as to why they were not met at Muscle Shoals. All now accepted that life on the frontier was uncertain. Henderson confirmed that they were, indeed, on the Cumberland River, although they probably would need another three to four weeks at their rate of progress to reach the settlement.

All of the Renfros gathered around Joseph's cooking fire. Olive was first to speak, "We have been through Hades itself, and we are still as far away as when we started. Only this time it's all upstream. The Lord must have His reasons. I wish I could understand it all."

"There is good news," chimed in Moses. "Captain Henderson told me the landmark to look for at the Red River. It's a high bluff called Red Rock Hill. He said it was unmistakable."

41

"What will we eat when we get there?" Joseph said despondently. "My wife packed enough food to get us through 'til the first crop came in. Most of it is gone. Even though it was the agreement, we couldn't let our neighbors starve. Everyone is out of bread and the meal to make it. We must keep our seeds at any cost."

"Joseph is right," acknowledged James. "We have to have the seeds. We could go on to the Cumberland with the others and return later."

Moses was emphatic: "I say we claim the land while we can. If we tarry, someone might get there before us. First possession is important."

After looking into the coals of the dying fire for awhile, a thought came to Joseph. "What about Isaac? Surely he started overland by now. Swine and cattle will not slow him. He should arrive there any day. Captain Henderson can tell him how to find us."

Richard Henderson took his leave, promising to remember all the messages to husbands and sons. He assured Moses Renfro that help of some form would be sent to him on the Red River as soon as possible.

While the Renfros were meeting, Bob was having a conversation with Prometheus, Rufus, and Jack Civil. "I tell you I've seen 'em do it," argued Jack.

"It's worth a try. I'll speak to Master Renfro."

Bob approached Joseph. "Master Renfro, Jack Civil say he know a way to hunt deer at night. He seen the Indians do it."

"Everybody about had their fill of buffalo and fish," Joseph agreed. "Whatever it is, we'll try it."

The moonless night appeared to be perfect to implement the hunting technique. Jack and Bob were in the lead canoe; Joseph and his son Billy followed in a second canoe. Joseph had noted in his heart how his son had grown with increased responsibility. Now, it was time for Billy to begin the rites of passage to manhood. His mother did not protest. They had a raft piled with twigs and dry wood floating in front tethered to Bob and Jack's canoe. After they had gone a short way, they stopped to light the wood on the raft. It blazed and reflected in the water like a beacon while floating slowly downstream. The hunters watched in amazement as deer walked to the river's edge and stared at the fire. Less than two hours later they returned with four deer. Even though it was late, the cooking fires were rekindled, as were their spirits, and the feast began. The method proved successful night after night. Even more, it eliminated the time consuming stalking of the deer. Captain Donelson opined as he filled his plate with venison that no gentleman would hunt deer in such a fashion. A slave and a freeman of color feeding his people did not merit a journal entry.

Their most pressing need taken care of, Ann Johnston once again resumed classes for the youngsters, and young Rachel made attempts to include Bob in the learning process. It was more difficult because of the work required to move the flotilla upstream. Bob and Rachel had little opportunity for conversation. A change came when Captain Donelson made a makeshift sail that improved his boat's handling and speed. Others who had the materials followed the example. Among the items Joseph had traded skins for was canvas. *Paradise Bound* responded as though she was made for sail. She could easily out-distance the other boats but stayed close for safety's sake. Rachel was allowed to resume occasional visits to the Renfro's boat.

Bob was manning the tiller. The breeze was gentle so the sail had been secured to the boat with no fear of it being ripped. For the first time in this new land, they enjoyed the splendor of nature. The riverbanks were covered in redbud and dogwood trees in full bloom. The display of red and white against the green background and blue sky was breathtaking. On the ground were flowers, mostly purple and yellow. Small birds of infinite variety and color hopped among the branches. Huge herons and other water birds fished in the shallows. Overhead, vultures, hawks, and eagles soared, riding the wind currents. Even Olive Renfro remarked that there was hope for this land after all. The Renfros were taking a well-deserved rest. Rachel moved closer to Bob for ease of conversation.

"My father says all of you will be leaving us soon."

"Anytime now from what I hear. We lookin' for a little river that Cap'n Henderson said was ten or twelve days from where we met him. Master Moses gonna have his own country there, with him as the ruler."

"It won't be exactly like that. Every place has to have a leader."

"Ole Pharaoh Renfro. That is a good name for him."

"Bob, don't you let anyone hear you say that. You'll be in big trouble."

"I'm always careful Missy. I just jokin' with you."

Joseph Renfro had been dozing near where he had tied off the sail. Overhearing this part of the conversation, he opened one eye as if to say,

"I think the name fits too." He smiled in contentment, closed the eye, and dozed off again.

"Bob," Rachel hesitated, "I'll always remember you. You saved my life. You helped feed us all. Patsy says you are the best boy she ever knew. I agree with her. I will always include you in my prayers. And who knows? Maybe we'll meet again. Like Miss Olive always says, 'The Lord works in mysterious ways.'"

Bob was unsure how to respond to the young lady. He had a strong feeling for her. He wanted to protect her always. Suddenly, he leaped to his feet. "Red Paint Hill! Red Paint Hill!"

VI

On Wednesday, April 12, 1780, the Renfro Company, including the families of Moses, James, and Joseph, along with Solomon and Nathan Turpin, bid farewell to the Donelson Party and started up the Red River. There would be no sails used on this narrow body of water. The Red was a peacefully flowing river and progress was steady. On the second day, Moses surveyed the land along a little creek. The land appeared perfect; it was flat and much of it bare of trees, as though it had been farmed before. Just beyond the clearing, the forest was filled with the tulip poplar trees they would use for their homes. This was to be the site of Renfro Station.

The first order of business was to build an enclosure for protection. It took most of a week for the five men and their three slaves to fell trees and construct a small stockade. Trapping small game and hunting kept them in food, and Olive still managed to bring forth small quantities of dried beans. On the first hunt, Bob saw signs of bear and made plans to get one at the first opportunity. The women and children busied themselves moving supplies from the boats and preparing the sites for cabins. The boat sail became part of a temporary shelter, and the fateful day came when it was time to dismantle *Paradise Bound*. The lumber was needed to make their home. Bob, Joseph, and Billy paused reverently before their task.

"She was the finest boat of them all," Joseph proclaimed

Bob agreed, "Yes, suh, she be that. Been our home for a long time."

"Papa, what happens if we need a boat or want to leave here?" Billy asked, wanting to give the boat a reprieve.

"Son, I won't leave here in this life. This is our new home. We'll travel overland on foot. Before too long we'll have horses. If absolutely necessary, we can travel by canoe." Joseph would have liked to save the boat too. He took one last look then added, "Bob, we need to do this carefully so we don't split the boards."

"Yes, suh, I be careful."

The necessity of the carrying on of life on the frontier removed any further sentiment from the task. The boat was soon dismantled and moved to the station, where it became the roofing on a small log cabin. Precious nails and spikes were saved and hoarded. The flatboats were taken apart for their lumber too. The dismantling of the boats came none too soon, for they witnessed how violent the little river could be after a downpour. The muddy water roared through, barely contained in its banks, pushing the tree limbs and trunks that had accumulated since the last storm. The force of the rushing water and the debris would destroy anything in its path. Luckily, Prometheus noticed the fast-rising water and awakened Bob and Rufus. The three black men were sharing a lean-to built against the station's newly constructed wall. They scrambled down the muddy banks and saved the canoes that had been left casually on the river's bank.

Shortly after the enclosure was completed, new settlers arrived. It had taken Donelson another twelve days to reach James Robertson's Cumberland Settlement. Richard Henderson had alerted the settlement to expect their arrival. The families of Isaac Renfro, Isaac Mayfield, James

Hollis, James Johns, and Abraham Jones more than doubled the Red River population. Isaac told his brothers that after Henderson told him they were alive, he had waited for Captain Donelson to confirm where they were and what they needed. They brought with them much needed supplies. Bread was again to be had and enjoyed. Potatoes and dried beans were again on their plates. Forest fruits and berries were being discovered. The promise and optimism that comes with spring was going to be fulfilled. Life was already improving at Renfro Station.

FOUR
RENFRO STATION –1780

Additional ground was cleared; the staples of life were planted. Corn, beans, squash, and potatoes were to be their main crops. James Robertson had named his fort, Fort Nashborough. A trail had been blazed through Kentucky, and frequent use would turn it into a well-worn path. In time wagons loaded with supplies would be in use. On May 13, 1780, the men of Fort Nashborough signed the articles of the "Compact of Government." Two hundred and fifty-five men put their signatures, and one man made his mark to a document establishing civil government and the rule of law. Isaac Renfro and Solomon Turpin were among them. Rights and privileges were now in place for the free people in all the settlements along the Cumberland.

Smaller fortifications, generally referred to as stations, were being built about a day's travel from the main fort in every direction. The male inhabitants from Renfro Station made regular trips to Eaton Station, which was north of Fort Nashborough on the Cumberland. Another settlement, Freeland Station was between Eaton Station and Robertson's fort. Mansker Station was to the northeast. All were part of a system of communication and protection. Renfro Station was by far the most remote. During the last week of May, it was Joseph's turn to make the trip to Eaton Station. Bob and William accompanied him on his overland trip. Returning along the developing trail, they camped on the banks of a small meandering stream that flowed into the larger Sycamore Creek which in turn was a tributary to the Cumberland River. William's marksmanship added an elk to their stores.

Soon after returning home, Moses Renfro called Joseph aside.

"What's on your mind, Moses?"

"It's your African boy. I think he is mocking me."

"Has he been disrespectful?"

"No. It's not that. I can't put my finger on it. He smiles too much. I am sure that he is having some joke at my expense. Elizabeth has noticed it too."

"Moses, with all due respect to you as my older brother and leader of this station, you, sir, are a pompous ass. My man Bob has contributed as much or more to this endeavor than anyone else. And you want me to stop him from smiling! If you ask me, we all need something to make us not only smile, but also laugh out loud."

With that pronouncement, Joseph turned and walked away, smiling to himself, "So there, Master Pharaoh."

Late that evening the Joseph Renfro family was sitting about an open fire. Olive Renfro had produced a stew combining several meats and a variety of vegetables. Most of the meats were bits and pieces left over from previous days. Mrs. Renfro, ever watchful of wastefulness, decided that all these leftovers would make a meal, so she just put it all together in one cast iron pot. Meat, potatoes, onions, corn, and whatever else came into her view went in the pot. It made a tasty and filling meal with the little fried cornmeal cakes. Bob was enjoying a bowl just outside the family circle.

"Bob, move on up closer to the fire," Joseph commanded. "We need to do some planning."

As Bob moved toward the circle, Sarah and Susan giggled in a girlish manner and shuffled to make room between them. They had known Bob all their young lives and were still unaware of any social taboos on association. Billy now regarded Bob as a companion. On the frontier, Joseph and Olive no longer cared how it was done "back East."

Joseph began his assessment of their current situation: "Our crops are planted. We'll have to work to keep the weeds out. Now its time to start preparing our winter meat. We need to build a little smokehouse. That shouldn't take long. We know from the river voyage that there is no such thing as too much food."

"Yes, suh, Master Renfro, we..."

"And that's another thing, stop calling me Master. Mister Joseph is sufficient."

"And I shall be Miss Olive"

"I thanks you both," a gracious Bob said.

"What were you going to say, Bob?"

"Well, Mister Joseph. We can get bear if'n we can use Mister Isaac's dog. Bear gives us more than any other animal. It just harder to get."

"Harder and more dangerous," Olive spoke forcefully. "I don't want William going on a bear hunt just yet." Olive knew that the use of the formal name would add emphasis to her order.

"Aw, Mother, I can do it."

"Son, you listen to your mother. There will be plenty of time and bears to hunt."

Olive sought to soften her stance. "I would like for you men to bring in more elk. They are larger than deer and just as tasty."

"How 'bout me and Mister William going out early tomorrow for that elk. Huntin' be best 'fore the sun get too high."

Bob and William were aware that in a short space of time they had moved up another notch in status. Though not quite as far up as young Mister William would have liked. Bob also started to refer to the girls as "Miss," for in his mind growing girls deserved as much respect as growing boys.

William accompanied Bob on many hunting expeditions. They were generally successful. The smokehouse was beginning to fill as the end of June approached. Jerky was being dried and animal skins were being stretched and tanned. Crops were doing well in the rich soil of the river bottom. New cabins were constructed around the perimeter of the stockade. The utopia promised by James Robertson was taking shape.

The attack took place without warning. An arrow went through Isaac Renfro's hound before it could raise an alarm. Choctaw and Chickasaw warriors sprang from the woods in front of Renfro Station. The painted braves were through the open gate before anyone could react. Nathan Turpin was the first to fall mortally wounded. The Indians were in the stockade destroying everything in sight as the people scattered in mass confusion. Men had to retrieve their rifles and ammunition before they could go into action. The long period without seeing hostile Indians in the area had made them complacent, so their weapons were not at hand.

Prometheus rushed to the defense of an unconscious Elizabeth Renfro. A warrior had her by the hair and was about take her scalp when Prometheus grabbed him by the throat and literally crushed his neck. He managed to take another's tomahawk. Wounded and dead Indians were piling up near the big man before he was shot through the chest. Several Indians fell on him hacking at him with their tomahawks.

Bob, Joseph, and William managed to get their rifles and started a steady, deadly volley on the warriors nearest to their cabin where Olive, Susan, and Sarah had managed to get inside and bar the door. Joseph fought his way to the cabin. Wounded Indians, aided by their companions, began an organized retreat, collecting their dead as they went.

The settlement was in shambles. Olive looked at the burning smokehouse. This was the end of her strength and her will. "Joseph, we must leave this place! In God's will, this was not meant to be. From the beginning, all the signs we were given told us that this was an accursed land. We put our faith in men, and they were wrong."

Neither Joseph nor anyone else could argue with her logic. Everything was gone. All their hard work was for naught. Their homes were burning; their fields had been trampled; horses had been taken off; cattle and swine had been killed; and the remaining canoes had been scuttled.

Moses Renfro took charge. "We are too short-handed to make another stand. James and Isaac won't be back for at least two days. Gather the things you can carry. We will leave first thing tomorrow morning. Maybe we can come back later with more men and retrieve our belongings."

A weary Joseph spoke to Bob, "Get together as much food, powder, and shot as we can carry. I don't think there is anything else here we want."

During the night the community helped Solomon Turpin bury Nathan. Nearby, Bob and Rufus with the help of Joseph and William Renfro dug a shallow grave for Prometheus and placed stones on it to keep animals out.

The next morning the task of leaving was difficult to get started. Many could not determine what they would carry. They packed and repacked. The bundles to be carried by Olive, Sarah, and Susan contained the beautiful coats Bob had made them; they were the one luxury Olive would consent to taking. Joseph, William, and Bob were to carry backpacks and bundles of food—mostly jerky—and their weapons. The departing members of Renfro Station stopped for a brief prayer. They asked only for divine protection. Even Olive Renfro could not find anything to be thankful for. The sun had been up almost three hours before they actually departed.

The group hadn't traveled far when some started to lament the personal possessions they left behind. Perhaps they were too hasty and should rethink this. This wasn't the first time they had to fight Indians. The bickering slowed their progress, but Joseph was unyielding in his decision: "We are going to Eaton Station, then to Fort Nashborough, and as soon as I can put it together, my family is returning to Virginia."

As midday approached they paused on the banks of a small creek, near the spot Joseph and Bob had selected when they took William with them to Eaton Station. A few families were still determined to return for more of their possessions. Moses approached Joseph.

"I'm at my wit's end," Moses said. "Some think I'm being too hasty, but I'm not going back. Elizabeth has suffered too much and I must get her to where she feels safe."

"I think we should go on too," confirmed Joseph. "My girls need a little rest; then we're ready to travel."

"That's just my point," said Moses. "I want to hurry. We've got six or seven hours of daylight left. How about you taking charge here? I'll take Elizabeth and a few men and move on. I can reach Freeland Station tomorrow."

"Do you think splitting up is a good idea?" asked Joseph. "There may still be savages about."

Moses tried to be convincing, "I think we gave them more than they reckoned for and they have retreated. They'll lick their wounds several days before trying another attack. We're not that far from Eaton Station. Go there first; then come on to Freeland's."

"Brother," Joseph said, "I still don't think splitting up is a good idea; however, we've followed you this far, so I'll do as you ask. I'll wait here while Jones and those other fools go back for their belongings. We'll be along in a day or two."

Isaac Mayfield, Solomon Turpin and a dozen others left with Moses Renfro. Staying behind were about fifteen individuals, including several children. Joseph called them together. "We'll wait here for those of you who want to retrieve more of your belongings. Don't be long about it. I want to leave here at first light tomorrow," he told the group. "My advice is to take only those who can travel fast. Mister Jones, you take charge of this group."

Abraham Jones and his companions began to retrace their steps. Jones's wife, Thelma, stayed with the main body. Joseph ordered William and Bob to stand guard and that no fires be lit. Olive was not pleased with the arrangement, but conceded that her daughters were slow travelers and "poor Elizabeth" needed to be taken to safety as soon as possible.

Half of the retrieval party returned late that same night. Sunrise came and the stragglers from Jones's party had not arrived. Joseph, in disgust, picked up a bucket and went to the creek. He would never return.

Bob went to search and returned minutes later. He whispered, "Miss Olive, Mister Joseph is dead. The Indians have murdered him."

Tears welled in Olive's eyes. "Dead?" she uttered.

"Yes 'um. Miss Olive, we got to take the chill'un and leave. Those redskins are all 'round us and gonna attack."

"Attack? My husband dead? What are you saying?" Olive gave a blank stare to Bob, and then looked around to her children. "Yes, we must save the children." She controlled the pain she felt as she regained her composure.

Olive went to Jones. "We must move on. Joseph has been murdered. We can't wait here for the rest of us to be killed," she pleaded.

"What makes you think Joseph is dead?" A disbelieving Jones asked.

"Our man Bob has seen what is left of his body. I tell you we must leave now!"

"We will wait until the others return. We need their guns," a shaken Jones replied.

Bob, for the first time he could remember since being a small boy, put his hands on Olive Renfro. He had her by the wrist. "I tell you Miss Olive, we will be kilt for sure if'n we stay."

Olive took command. "William, get Sarah. Susan, come with me."

Olive moved rapidly in the direction Bob indicated, crouching over to make herself less visible. She had her children; nothing else mattered. Left behind were the bundles containing their coats and Olive's Bible. They never looked back, as they set out on the trail Bob and William knew led to Eaton Station, pausing only briefly for rest now and then. William watched over the women while Bob scouted ahead. Distant rifle shots were heard from the direction they had just come. The shooting lasted only a brief time. Bob and Olive exchanged a worried glance, then moved on. Bob saw signs of Indians and was sure he heard them once. The travelers hid in the weeds until they were certain the danger had passed. They paused long enough to eat some of the jerky that Bob and William had tucked in their hunting shirts.

"Miss Sarah, Miss Susan," Bob was speaking in a hushed voice, "I know you tired, but we gots to move on. Mister William will help you. Miss

Olive, we be better off to rest in the daytime. Those redskins can sneak up on you at night. We can't build no fires."

Olive was as stunned and numb as her daughters. She nodded her agreement. They moved on slowly; late June provided no moonlight. At daybreak they felt safe enough to take a brief rest. After a couple of hours, Bob picked up Susan, and Olive picked up the smaller, still-sleeping Sarah. William had reached his manhood overnight. He took up his rifle and began to scout ahead. Late in the evening, they came to Eaton Station.

It was confirmed that Moses Renfro and his party had passed through, purchased a horse, and had continued on to Freeland Station. It had not been mentioned that a relief force should be sent to Joseph Renfro. No one had seen any signs of a large war party.

About noon the next day, a pale, bloody, and nearly nude woman emerged from the same trail. It was Thelma Jones. She was near hysteria but confirmed the worst. Those that remained had been massacred along the banks of the creek. She had escaped by running and stumbling along the trail used by Bob and Olive Renfro's family, the brush and briars ripping at her clothes and skin as she went.

A despondent Olive spoke, "Bob, I have always believed that the Lord would provide. Now, I don't know. You must help me to take care of my family."

"Yes 'um. You's all my family too."

FIVE
THE CUMBERLAND SETTLEMENT –1780

Men from Eaton Station made an attempt to go to the aid of Moses Renfro's abandoned party, but they encountered the same savages and had to fight their way back to the station. They reported that men, women, and children had been butchered beyond recognition. Olive and Thelma offered comfort to each other. Though they were in shock, the instincts of motherhood over came Olive's grief. Her children's survival was all that mattered. She resolved to go to Freeland Station and then on to Fort Nashborough. She wanted to be where the most protection was offered for her family. Fort Nashbrough, more generally referred to as "The Bluffs," was situated on high bluffs above the river where the Cumberland flows to the northwest. Less than a mile to the south, the river made an oxbow curve. The Cumberland's headwaters were in the mountains of Eastern Kentucky. It flowed southwest until it made this big bend and then flowed back across Western Kentucky into the Ohio.

Moses Renfro avoided contact with Olive as he struggled with his conscience over having left them behind. It took what was left of Olive's resolve to be cordial to Charlotte Robertson, whom she felt was the one whose argument convinced her to make the journey, and it was Charlotte's husband, by now known as "Colonel" Robertson, whose glorious description of the peaceful land had persuaded everyone else. She prayed hard to adopt the position that it was God's will. Then too, the people of the Cumberland Settlement had their own problems with Indians. Scarcely a day went by that news did not arrive of some unfortunate soul being caught and slaughtered by "murdering heathens." Widows and orphans were accumulating at a rapid rate. Ann Johnston organized the women. "We must be prepared to defend this place. There should never be a time that one of us is not in the watchtower day and night. What can we do if the barbarians attack the walls? I've read stories of how people in Europe poured scalding water and oil out of the castles onto their attackers. I think, too, we should train hounds to smell Indians and attack them."

Olive volunteered her services in any way possible. She admired the young widow, and knew that if there was a woman strong-willed enough to lead them, it was Ann Johnston. The two women concluded it would be easier if they joined their households. Olive's older girls would help look after Ann's youngsters. The women set to their task while the men were busy with clearing and breaking new ground around the settlement. Hunting parties had to continue to go out.

Olive was almost apologetic when she said, "Bob, I'm afraid I have doubled your burden. You are hunting game for two families. Joseph's kinsmen and others will help us. After all, Miss Ann is Colonel Robertson's sister, but all have their own families to think about, and we know all too well that they think about themselves first. Another thing, I may have to hire you out some. Maybe working on shares, you can earn enough to keep us clothed and fed. I'll try to make sure it's not for long at a time. I cannot do without you very long. This much I do say: 'I will never sell you. You will be a Renfro as long as you live.'"

From that moment on, Bob considered himself to be Bob Renfro.

Olive started to leave but then turned back, "One more thing. I don't want William to hunt unless it's with a big party. You understand?"

"Yes 'um. I know what to do. It not much different than what I been doin'. 'Bout Mister William. You ain't gonna keep that young man tied down long. He done tasted what it be like to do for himself. He think he be a proven man."

"You're right, of course, but I'm still his mother."

Word came of the problems that had befallen the Donelsons. They had gone east to the Stones River's fertile bottomland they named Clover Bottom and planted corn and cotton. Mary Purnell Donelson had a son christened Chised. They had to fight off Indians. In July, the much prayed for rains came, and the Stones River flooded covering Clover Bottom. The Donelsons were homeless and retreated into Mansker Station. A passerby came with the news that the corn they had planted was coming in. The decision was made to harvest it. It was just too valuable to let go. John Donelson, Jr., organized a party to work on shares. Men from the Bluffs were offered half the cornfield if they joined the harvest. Olive immediately decided that this was a good place to send Bob, and she let William accompany him. Bob went eagerly hoping to hear about the welfare of Rachel. A handful of men and slaves joined the Bluff party, poling a boat the ten miles upstream to Clover Bottom. Accompanying Donelson on a boat from Mansker's were the Donelson's man Jim, Jack Civil, and a family of five named Gower.

The corn was successfully gathered. Donelson's boat and the boat from the Bluff were loaded. Ignoring a warning to stay together, the Gower family cast off the lines and began floating down the Stones River. Almost immediately, the Indian attack began. The Gowers were hapless and died in the onslaught. The Bluff party rallied around Bob and William. They were known survivors. Donelson and Jim disappeared into the canes along the riverbank. Jack Civil was seen being carried off by the attackers. Blacks and horses were in the same category for Indians: They were valuable as a means of exchange between themselves and whites.

The Bluff boat had to be abandoned. The survivors started to make their way toward the Cumberland, and they managed to make the big bend of the river without further incident. They hiked back empty-handed to the fort. Soon after, word came that Donelson and Jim managed to escape and that the Donelsons were leaving for Kentucky. Most of the Renfros were leaving as well. Olive was beside herself with anger. "The very men who led us here are abandoning us! I thought John Donelson was made of better stuff," she shouted in disbelief. "My family will not follow him and Moses Renfro another step. My husband's dream is here, and here we will stay." She spoke to the walls, for nobody else was around. It came to her that over sixty of those who left Fort Patrick Henry only nine months ago were now dead. With the departure of the Donelsons and most of the Renfros, less than half of the original party was left. "We were bound for paradise then. Has God truly abandoned us? Are we the new banished children of Eden?"

Some good news arrived in late fall. Colonel John Sevier and Colonel Isaac Shelby had taken the men from the western side of the mountains, including those from Fort Patrick Henry, across the mountains into North and South Carolina. There, these Overmountain Men defeated the British at a battle on King's Mountain, killing the British commander. With this news, James Renfro concluded that the world was passing him by. His real place was with the militia, fighting the British. Olive reluctantly bid farewell to her husband's last relative in Cumberland Settlements and her ties to the Renfro family.

There were several hundred men in the Cumberland Settlement area. While the Donelson Party was struggling on the rivers, overland parties were arriving regularly. There was one thing that Olive had not reckoned with: On the frontier, unmarried women were in short supply. Even widows with children were much courted; there was no such thing as a decent interval to grieve. Suitors for two handsome ladies did not come empty handed. They usually brought Olive and Ann something for the cooking pot in the hopes of being invited to stay for dinner. Among the suitors, Randall Smith was particularly proficient at hunting turkey and shared his knowledge and hunting hounds with Bob and William. Bob appreciated this system of courting. At least he didn't have to hunt everyday. William, on the other hand, didn't like the system much. "I can take care of my mother myself," he complained to Bob. "We don't need them coming around all the time."

Bob explained, "Now Mister William, we all need a little help from time to time. Your maw can take care of herself. Ever'thing gonna be all right."

Bob was adding to his storehouse of knowledge. He already knew about tracking, stalking, killing, skinning, butchering, drying, smoking, and storing animals. Now he was proficient in felling trees and building cabins. His boat building knowledge came in handy. He knew three different ways to notch logs to make corner joints. He could bore holes and drive pegs. He could split rails, and he could make boards. He learned about the grinding of corn and all that could be done with it. Old Patsy's advice continued to be borne out: "You got to take your time to make it fit to eat."

Someone had to take care of the horses. They could not be left outside the walls because Indians were always on the lookout for an opportunity to steal a horse. Cattle and hogs could be left close-by behind split rail fences since driving them was too slow for the marauding savages. Killing or maiming these animals was the more likely threat. Stables had to be mucked out daily. The manure had to be carted out and spread for drying so it could be used as fertilizer. Bob and William agreed they would be part of the rotation if they could have occasional use of the horses and hunting hounds. The price of a horse was beyond what they could hope to earn.

The cornfield was also community property. All were expected to take their turn tending the crop. Weeding the corn was a constant. Of all the chores, Bob disliked the laborious and boring task of hoeing the garden the most.

By the time of the first heavy frost, the harvest was done. The trees on the banks of the Cumberland were glorious in their fall foliage. Brilliant shades of red, orange, and yellow harmonized with the greens and browns. Once more a secure feeling was taking over although Indian attacks had not ceased. Indians were also busy preparing for the coming of winter. By the end of November, the storehouses were full. Smokehouses contained an abundance of meat. Additional fresh meat could be obtained through hunting, as the supply of small game was never-ending. The river and streams yielded fish with the slightest effort. Bob and William had contributed their share as well. Bob had again shown his ability to trade. He bartered and swapped with other slaves and coached William in deal-making with whites. Skins for cover and clothes would be no problem. Over an acre of chopped wood stacked six-foot high was just outside the gate. Bob's lean-to was as snug as possible, covered in wall-to-wall furs.

Life slowed down in colder months. The winter was particularly hard with sleet as well as snow. It brought back the memories of last winter when the Holston and the Cumberland froze. "The frozen river was the first sign we ignored. Then the gates of hell opened and we fell through," Olive thought.

In January, Charlotte Robertson's son Felix was born. He was the third male child to be born in the Cumberland, but he was the first born at The Bluffs. The presence of a baby kept all of the women occupied and gave them something to talk about. Olive and Ann continued to receive gentlemen callers. Their contribution to the meal was always acknowledged and appreciated.

Spring burst forth with all its promise. More fields were being cleared and planted. Early one April morning, three painted Indian braves emerged from the forest into the clearing before the fort. They moved to about half way and stopped. Remaining at two hundred and fifty yards, they knew they were out of rifle range. Men gathered on the wall to observe them. As the drama played out, a few women joined them. They gazed at the young bucks speculating on just what they were up to. Their eyes widened with astonishment when the braves dropped their deerskin pants and displayed their bare backsides to the fort. They wiggled and yelled to the amusement of some and the outrage of others. "We'll teach those heathens a lesson," someone bellowed as the men mounted horses and rushed out the gate. The Indians made for the forest.

Charlotte Robertson was taking her turn in the watchtower. Movement caught her attention. Warriors were massed in the woods. When the horsemen saw them, they reigned in their mounts, dismounted, and prepared to fight. The women's defense force went into action.

Charlotte commanded, "Ann, loose the hounds! Hurry!"

Ann Johnston opened the gate and gave her hounds the command to attack. About twenty hounds leaped through the gate and raced toward the Indians. Pandemonium reigned. Horses bolted, men cursed, Indians chased horses, and yelping hounds chased Indians. Five men from the fort were killed and three more wounded. In time all the horses were recovered. What was most remembered about the day was that women and hounds had saved the impetuous men of the fort. Of course, men remembered it as the day that some overly clever Indians tried to steal their horses. Bob and William had been in some horrible fights with these savages and were having trouble digesting what they witnessed that day. "You know, Mister William," Bob said. "If not for the dead, what we saw toda'd be funny. It was just plain crazy. Twenty men chasing a few Indians 'cause they showed their backsides. They should have knowed it was some kind of trick. How you suppose Cur'nel Robertson get tricked like that? It be a good thing these women got better heads on their shoulders than the men folk. We almost lost our horses. We near had to give up shovelin' manure."

II

A grim cycle of life took over the Cumberland Settlement. Survival was foremost in their minds. Colonel Robertson explained their situation, concluding, "We can fight our way out of here, or we can fight it out here." The resounding response, particularly from the women, was, "Fight it out here!" Olive saw little choice. Standing behind the fort's defensive wall seemed to be the better option. Food was meager, but ample. Eatable berries and nuts were gathered in season. Small game, particularly turkeys, became a staple. When turkeys went to roost, they could be shot out of the trees. Small game could be trapped. Dogs assisted in the hunting of everything. Still, hunting was dangerous because of the possibility of Indian attack. Bob and William had become so proficient at hunting that they were able to start a small trading operation. Mostly their trades consisted of getting out of their more distasteful chores. Hauling of manure and hoeing weeds became a thing of the past for these young entrepreneurs. They were the proud owners of two fine dogs purchased from Randall Smith, and at long last, Olive agreed that the evidence before her was too strong so William could hunt bear. Hunting with dogs added protection against Indian attack, both as a warning system and the fact that the Indians had become extremely frightened of the settlers' dogs.

Their hunting success didn't lessen the frequent male visitors to the Johnston-Renfro cabin although it did help to narrow the field. It seemed that Misters John Cockrell and James Shaw had their feet under the table more than others.

The population stayed about the same: A baby would be born, new immigrants would arrive, and Indians would kill one or two men. Ann Johnston continued to hold school. Every white child in the settlement could read and write. Books were available and well passed around, read, and reread. Bibles were in plentiful supply. Nightly Bible reading was a practice in most households. Olive's lost Bible had been replaced from the possessions of a fallen pioneer. Storytelling was enjoyed as a favorite. Bob was an acknowledged spinner of stories enjoyed by his fellow blacks and the families of Olive Renfro and Ann Johnston.

As they were putting aside their winter supplies in the fall of 1781, glorious news came. General George Washington had won a major battle. He and French allies had cut off and captured an entire British army at Yorktown in Virginia. It was the opinion of everyone that this would lead to the long dreamed of independence for the American colonies. Without the British to incite the Indians, it was hoped that the Indian attacks would cease. It was also determined that when the time came, the town would be known as Nashville. The use of "borough" was too British; "ville" would be used in tribute to the French who had been the Americans' ally in achieving independence. James Robertson had selected the name Nash in 1779 to honor his friend General Francis Nash of North Carolina, who had died in action fighting the British in Pennsylvania two years earlier.

With the end of hostilities in the East, new settlers made their way to Nashville. The State of North Carolina was rewarding her soldiers for their service with land grants in the west. Before these grants were made, the claims of the original settlers from the Transylvania Company were to be honored. Olive received her land when the heirs of Joseph Renfro were awarded preemptive rights to 640 acres along both sides of Richland Creek on the Red River. William received land nearby. The lands of Moses, Isaac, and James Renfro were included in the preemptions. One extraordinary land grant was made by the North Carolina legislature. Recognizing her exceptional contributions to the advancement of civilization, Ann Johnston was given a land grant, the only woman so honored. A mulatto man named David Gowan received 640 acres on the south side of the Cumberland. Unfortunately, Indians had killed Gowan at Manskers Station.

Jack Civil reappeared in the settlement. He boasted that he had escaped from the Indians who had captured him at Clover Bottom. He claimed that as a freeman he was entitled to a land grant. Others came forward and testified that Jack Civil was the negro seen in the company of Indians on raids against whites. Though Civil vehemently denied these charges, he was declared a known liar and denied a land grant. He was never seen in Nashville again.

The breaking up of the fortified settlement was inevitable. The frontier was being expanded. A town was laid out near where the old fort stood. Commissioners were appointed. A courthouse and jail were sure signs that their days of isolation were over. Olive decided she would marry James Shaw. Ann married John Cockrell. All of this progress meant little change to the way Bob conducted his life. He was more or less an independent contractor, hiring himself out to those in need of his services.

As an accomplished builder, he was always in demand. He turned over his earnings to Miss Olive, who in turn was generous with him, allowing him to keep anything she didn't need. He was accumulating wealth for which he had no need, yet he enjoyed the bartering process and accumulated even more, so much so that he constructed himself a little building with ample room for storage. Bob helped William clear part of his land. After a family council, it was determined that William Renfro should return to Virginia were he was to be educated and learn the ways of a gentleman. He and Bob had one last overnight hunt before their hunting hounds were to be sold. As they relaxed at their campfire, Bob began to rehash the past: "You r'member much about Virginny?"

"Not much. How about you?"

"Just what Ole Patsy told me. I thinks I 'member when I come to your Ma and Pa and we started moving. I was a little thing. Miss Olive always say, 'Come on, Bob, you going with us,' and I went. When I got bigger, Mister Joseph took me hunting with him and the other men. At first, I just built fires and skinned animals. Learned to cook some. Then Mister Joseph would go out, just me and him. You was sickly. Miss Olive was 'fraid for you to go. I learned to track, and he showed me how to shoot. There was always them murdering savages. I could read their signs too. Pretty soon your Papa say, 'Bob you take this rifle; it is yours.' 'Course I remember when your sisters was born."

"What I know about hunting I learned from you, Bob. We have sure had us some times."

"Yes, suh, we sho have. Good thing Miss Olive never found out 'bout some of our bear hunts, else you never hunt again and my black hide be stretched on her wall."

The two companions told their version of stories they both knew all to well because they had lived them together and rolled with laughter until they finally dozed off. The next morning as they were breaking camp, William fumbled for a way to express one more thing that was on his mind: "Bob, I don't know how long I'll be gone. Surely, as there is a God in Heaven, we will hunt again someday. One thing I've heard about the redskins I kind of like. If they really like someone, they become blood brothers. I'll always consider you my blood brother. Maybe we should do that, you know formal like."

Bob's eyes grew larger at the thought. "Now just you wait a minute Billyboy. Ole Bob is not all dat ready to be carving on his own carcass. 'Sides don't you think after all the fights and scrapes we been in, our blood has already mingled?"

"Yes, of course you're right. I was just thinking out loud."

SIX
CIVILIZATION

Olive Shaw adapted to her new station in life. She was among the elite of Nashville and by most standards a wealthy woman. She and her husband had vast landholdings. Olive determined that she could look out for herself. She became quite a businesswoman, managing her own lands and William's property as well. Infringement on Olive Shaw's property meant an immediate appearance before the newly established Committee of the Cumberland Association, as Frederick Stump found when he planted corn on land cleared by William Renfro. Stump agreed to pay a reasonable rent in corn, and the case was dismissed. Olive began to buy and sell lots in the newly established town.

Bob was Olive's most valuable asset. He was well-known throughout the community. Nobody questioned his comings and goings. At times, Olive would inform him that she had hired him out; at other times, he made the deal himself. He kept his mistress informed of his whereabouts and turned over the profits. Bob built himself a cabin on the outskirts of the new town and traded for a few pieces of furniture. A table, two chairs, and a rope bed furnished his dwelling. Placing a few furs over the ropes made it very comfortable to sleep on. The community, in order to make sure he was not confused with any other Bob, started to refer to him as "Black Bob."

One of Bob's frequent jobs involved the grinding of corn. Some corn was ground using a device known as a hominy pounder. Grains of corn were placed into a partially hollowed out log. The inside had a taper to it. On the end of a long pole was a weighted pestle, a smaller log with a sharpened end to fit into the tapered log. This was the pounder. The pounder-pole pivoted on a center post. The pounder was raised and allowed to fall on the corn. After numerous poundings the corn would be broken into a course meal. Another method was grinding stones. Olive was fond of pointing out that it was the way it was done in the Bible. A water driven gristmill was built near the old Eaton's Station. All methods required a lot of human labor. The corn had to be shucked, the kernels removed from the cob and fed into the mill, and the cornmeal collected. The meal could then be used in a variety of ways, from making bread to adding hot water in order to make a mush called grits. A little bear grease added to the mixture made it excellent for frying and very tasty.

A fortuitous accident caused by a sudden thunderstorm prompted Bob to seek some advice. Several sacks of meal got wet, more than could possibly be used before it spoiled. "Take it to Old Man Cunningham. He just built a still," Joseph Paisley advised him. As a result Bob was introduced to the art of making corn whiskey. Whiskey making was a lengthy process, but the results could be very profitable. Mister Cunningham needed a man like Bob. There was wood to be cut, fires to be tended, and a mixture to be made known as "mash," which was allowed to ferment. The fermented mash was heated to cause a vapor that was trapped in a copper coil for condensation. A clear liquid dripped out of the coil and was collected in jugs and wooden kegs. "To make it right, you got to take your time," was Cunningham's admonition. "Ain't no hurrying this process."

"Yes, suh," Bob grinned. "Seems to me I heard that somewhere befo'."

Bob worked for several people who had stills, learning a little from each one. Each had his own technique that made his brew different and sometimes better. "Add a little of this," "not so much of that," "keep the fire low," "make it hotter," "good water," "any water," "don't use sulfur water," although some said that using sulfur water would make a foul-tasting medicine that would aid in the recovery of most illnesses. Bob listened and learned and determined that someday he would get his own still and make the best whiskey in Nashville. Bob took several jugs given him as his share and poured them in a single keg that he placed in the corner of his cabin. It was a good place to set his candle so that it wasn't likely to turn over.

The sun shone brightly on a late spring day in 1785. Bob thought he recognized a man standing near the old fort. "Mister Johnny Donelson, is that you?"

"Well, hello, Bob. Yes, it's me. I just got back from Kentucky."

"It sure be good to see you. How be your ma and pa and Miss Rachel?"

"Mother is here too. She's staying with the Robertsons. Father will join us soon. My sister stayed in Kentucky. She recently married a man named Lewis Robards."

Bob was disappointed that he would not get to see Miss Rachel. He tried to imagine her all growed up and with a husband too. Maybe chill'uns soon. "Well, suh, maybe she visit soon. You tell 'em all, Ole Bob remember them with respect."

"I'll do that. I must be off to see Colonel Robertson. He is helping arrange to have a suitable dwelling built."

Bob was immediately hired to help build a home for John Donelson. They had scarcely gotten the foundation in place when the news arrived that Colonel John Donelson was dead. He had been killed when he and two companions had been attacked along the Barren River. Rumors circulated that it was not an Indian attack, as claimed, but murder. No proof could be established to support such a claim.

Rachel Donelson Robards made the overland journey from Kentucky to Nashville to be with her recently widowed mother. Returning to a land that she had left as a thirteen-year-old girl, now she was a stunningly beautiful young woman. She saw Bob when she visited the site where the home was being constructed.

"Bob, you haven't changed a bit."

"You sho have, Missy. You all growed up. You a sight for Ole Bob's eyes. It just does a body good to see you."

"You can stop that old nonsense. How have you been?"

"Oh, just fine. Mistress Shaw treat me just fine. I gots my own place."

"Yes, I intend to talk to her before I go back to my husband in Kentucky."

Rachel had her opportunity to speak with Olive Shaw when several of the ladies of Nashville called on the widow and her daughter at the Robertson home.

"Rachel, child, marriage seems to agree with you."

"Yes, Mrs. Shaw, I'm very happy."

"Please dear, call me Olive."

"Thank you, Miss Olive, and how are your children?"

"All in Virginia. William is studying law now, and I sent my daughters back for finishing school. After all these years, I still don't feel they are safe here."

After the social amenities of the day were over, Rachel sought out a private conversation with Olive.

"Miss Olive, I've heard the stories of how you and your children escaped after the Indian attacks that killed Mister Renfro."

"Yes, again the Lord moved in a mysterious way. We couldn't have been gone more than two hours when the last attack took place."

"Your man Bob, he saved me from the river and then saved you and your family. Has he been suitably…"

Before Rachel could get the word "rewarded" out, Olive interrupted, "Yes, Bob was very helpful. And he has helped out so much since. Excuse me, I must speak with Charlotte." Olive remembered what Rachel had said after Bob had rescued her, but she did not want to think about it at this time.

Rachel stood with her mouth half opened, thinking, "What is wrong with that woman? She knew I was going to remind her that Bob should have his freedom, and she cut me off. Has she changed that much? From all that I've heard, Bob kept them all alive and fed until she married Mister Shaw. The Shaws increase their holdings daily, and still she wants to keep Bob as her property."

Rachel left Nashville without seeing Olive Shaw again. Olive gave passing thought as to what she might do with Bob when she obtained the legal authority to administer the estate of her late husband, Joseph Renfro. She concluded Bob was just too valuable to make any rash decisions. She would think and pray on it for a while longer. She could not explain the feeling of security she felt just by knowing Bob was hers. After sometime she made the only compromise her conscience would permit. She sent for Bob.

"Bob, the laws of this settlement do not permit me to just set you free; however, you are free to come and go as you please. You can also keep the fruits of your labor. When the law changes, we'll talk about this again. You understand that you are still my property?"

"Yes 'um. I thinks I understand." He paused then and looked her in the eyes, "Miss Olive, *all* people wants to be free. I thank you most kindly. If you or any of Mister Joseph's people ever need me, all you have to do is send word and you knows Ole Bob come-a-runnin'."

II

With his newfound "freedom" Bob didn't change much. He continued to earn and accumulate. He most liked spending time with Old Man Cunningham. The elder man told him stories of making whiskey using different grains. Bob also spent a lot of his time at the new home of Widow Donelson. He especially enjoyed the company of Patsy, and she enjoyed instructing him on the proper way to cook. "Now that we got a proper cook house and proper cookin' stuff, I can make most anythin' I wants. We got flour and sugar too. I show you about bakin'. They need to git a girl in here to help me. We got one, but she always in the big house helpin' with somethin' else. So, you jist have to do. You ain't purdy, but you good help." She laughed out loud at her last remark.

Besides their common maxims, Bob noticed other similarities between what Patsy told him about cooking and what Mister Cunningham told him about making whiskey. The mixing, the heat, yeast in the starter, and "if'n you ain't got somethin', find a substitute." Patsy kept a bucket of wood that had been burnt down into charcoal. She said it was good to filter poison out of liquids, or "if'n you got a little pi'son in yo' system, you jist swallow a li'l of the grit and powder. It fix you right up."

In September of 1788 the Cumberland Road was extended to Nashville. The first wagon train was expected any day now. In late October, Bob was relaxing in his cabin when he answered a loud rapping on his door.

"Are you Bob?" asked the tall, lean stranger.

"Yes, suh, they calls me Black Bob. What can I do fer you?"

"I was expecting a man of color. A freeman. I was told a man named Bob could help me with my dilemma."

"I don't know what that dilemma mean. I ain't 'xactly free, but I the next best thing. Ain't I colored enough?"

"No, I meant…"

Bob knew what he meant. White folks had categories. If one had light colored skin he was called "colored." It was assumed that at least one parent, usually the father, was white, and sometimes the person was free. Bob knew a few men of color, but he wasn't one.

"I want to hire you to look after a sick girl."

"Sick girl? I don't know nothin''bout takin' care of sick people."

"Let me start over. My name is Andrew Jackson. I just arrived here with the wagon train. I have a negro girl who is sick. There is no place to take her. I'll pay you to let her stay here until she is well enough to look after herself."

"What be wrong with her? She got the pox or somethin'?"

"I don't think so. She is just ill and needs a place to rest. Are you for hire or not?"

"I can't turn away a sick girl. She can stay. I'll sleep outside."

Bob's mind was racing. "What have I done? I don't know nothin' about takin' care of a sick girl 'cept what Patsy done told me, and that ain't much."

Andrew Jackson led the young woman to Bob's cabin. "Her name is Annie. I'll check on her in a couple of days after I find a place to stay." With that, he left.

The girl, Annie, was too sick and too tired to be scared. She shuffled to Bob's bed; lay down, and promptly fell asleep. Bob put some cover over her and left the cabin. "What to do? What to do?" was all he could think of. He looked in on the girl from time to time, but she continued to sleep. "Make a broth!" came to him. "She'll need nourishment." So he busied himself making a broth by boiling venison and adding a few seasonings.

Two days later Andrew Jackson returned.

"Mister Jackson, that girl still sleepin'. She took a little broth and some sulfur medicine I makes. She ain't got no fever. Her breathin' seems to be all right. I think she gonna be well."

"That's good. When do you think that will be? I have a sizable investment in her."

Bob did not like what he heard. Was he getting the girl well so she could be sold? Who was this Andrew Jackson?

"Can't say. Just have to wait and see. You wants me to send fer you?"

"Well, I've taken up lodging at the Widow Rachel Donelson's place. I'll be here every day. I'm a lawyer. I have business here."

"You stayin' at Missus Donelson's? Across the river?"

"Yes, I am. In the blockhouse. You know the place?"

"Yes, suh. I helped build the house. I goes there reg'lar. I knows the cook."

"The cook! She seems a little old for you."

"Oh, no, suh, I didn't mean it that way. We just friends."

"Well, be that as it may, I have some business to attend to. I'll check on the girl's condition tomorrow."

That evening, Annie was feeling better. Bob fixed her a meal, and they ate together. She flatly refused another dose of Bob's sulfur medicine. She started to quiz him.

"You a strange man. You don't seem to have no master. How that be?"

"I've got a owner, Mistress Olive Shaw. She lets me do what I likes most of the time. But, she still my owner. Told me herself not to ever forget that. How you come to be with this Mister Lawyer Andrew Jackson?"

"He buy me jus' 'fore we j'ined the wagon train. I guess he thinks he can sell me here and make mo' money. That man is interested in makin' money and a name fer himself. He can't make no money while I be sick. Nobody want me."

"You a cook?"

"Not much; I do housework. White gen'lemen like me."

"He probably gonna sell you to that man at the *Red Heifer*."

"Red Heifer? It a tavern? I can do tavern work."

"Yes. But you won't like the owner. They calls him King Boyd. He a hard man. Runs a hard place. I done some work for him makin' corn whiskey. He treats me worse than anyone in this whole settlement. He just got a bad temper. I avoids him if'n I can."

The following day another young white visitor appeared at Bob's cabin.

"I am Bennett Searcy. Mister Jackson asked me to check on his property. He'll be by tomorrow."

"You mean the girl Annie?"

"Yes, of course. Is she well?"

"Ask her."

Bennett Searcy was to be the clerk at the new District Court. Judge John McNairy had appointed him and Andrew Jackson to act as the prosecuting lawyer. Searcy did not like being directed by a negro.

"I asked you a question. Answer it!"

"Yes, suh, I knows you did. The girl know better how she feel than I do. That why I say, 'ask her.'"

Bennett Searcy paused for a moment. Had this smiling black man outwitted him? "How are you, girl?"

"I be much improved. You tells Mister Jackson I ready."

Bennett Searcy left and made his report to Andrew Jackson. The following day Jackson came and took Annie away. A short time later he returned.

"Bob, I need to settle my account with you."

"Ain't no account Mister Jackson. The girl weren't no trouble. Didn't eat much. What I already had."

"I said I will pay you, and I will. Here are two dollars."

"Thank you, suh. I most 'preciative."

Andrew Jackson was a man with something on his mind. He just stood looking down his nose at the shorter black man before him. He didn't like negroes, but somehow this affable man puzzled and intrigued him.

Jackson spoke, "I understand you are known by Mistress Rachel Donelson Robards."

"Miss Rachel. I should say I is. I knowed her a long time. I was on the river with her family and the Renfros. Yes, suh. I knows Miss Rachel. You knows her too?"

"I just met her. She has come to visit her mother."

Bob took another long look at Lawyer Andrew Jackson. He had taken on a new disposition. He spoke Rachel's name in a soft tender way. It came to Bob, "This man is lightnin'. Thunder and a storm will surely follow."

III

Bob decided it was time he went to see Patsy. He knew it was just his excuse, for he really hoped that he would get to see Miss Rachel. He made sure Andrew Jackson was at the courthouse before he left.

Bob and Patsy had their usual discussion concerning the art of cooking. Patsy was explaining how to always have yeast on hand. "You can keep a little of what you be usin' to start som'thin' else, or you can dry it. You add some warm water, and it start workin' all over again. I give you some of the dried when you ready to go."

"I heared Miss Rachel was visitin' her ma."

"I wondered when you get 'round to askin' 'bout that child. She ain't happy with that man she done married."

"That ain't good. Who all livin' here now?"

"You askin' 'bout Mister John Overton and Mister Andrew Jackson. They share dat little place out back. Ole Miss Donelson feel safer with some mo' white menfolk 'round. You know you never can be too safe as long as dar still 'em red devils 'round. It ain't like she need the money. She still got land in Virginny and Kentuck. Ole Mister John had business all over the place." Patsy went on, "Dat Mister Jackson, I do believe be the skinniest man I ever see'd. He ain't big 'round as nothin'. I guess I just have to fatten 'em up."

"I knows Mister Jackson. He brought a sick girl to my place."

"That the girl that died?"

85

"Died?"

"Bob, I swear you have to git more black friends, else you never know nothin' 'bout what's goin' on. Mister Jackson was lettin' dat Boyd man work her at his whiskey place. She took sick and died overnight."

Before Bob and Patsy could discuss details, Rachel Robards came to the cookhouse. "Hello Bob. I thought it was you out here. How have you been?"

"Just fine, Miss Rachel. Mistress Shaw kind of set me free."

"Just what does 'kind of' mean?"

"Well, ma'm, she say that the law ain't ready to set me free. Have to be some new law. She say I can come and go as I please 'round here. If'n I leave, I be a run-a-way."

"New law? I'll have to ask Mister Overton and Mister Jackson about that. They are both lawyers."

Rachel was still seeking answers to her legal questions when her husband arrived hoping to persuade her to return to Kentucky with him. Rumor had it that Robards confronted Andrew Jackson concerning the attention Jackson was giving to Rachel. They had some strong words, and Jackson offered to duel him. Nothing came of it. Rachel and Lewis Robards reconciled, and she left with her husband.

IV

It was a cold and rainy day in December. Bob was at the courthouse talking with the man who cleaned the place. The courthouse and jail were little more than large cabins. The stocks for punishing minor crimes were nearby. Today, there was a young man with his head and arms firmly secured in the stocks. The weather had kept spectators away.

"Ain't they gonna let that boy out of the stock 'fore he catches his death," asked a concerned Bob.

"Don't know. Won't be much of a loss 'cause that boy ain't gonna 'mount to much anyway. Always in one kind of trouble or 'nother."

"Who is he? What did he do?"

"I think his name is Terrell, Malcolm Terrell—drunk and disorderly. If'n he don't learn his lesson this time he gonna die young."

Bob heard the call of Andrew Jackson, "Black Bob, I've been wanting to talk to you."

"Yes, suh. What can I do fer ya?"

"Is there some place we can talk?"

"We can go back to my place, if'n you like."

"I'll pick up a jug and come there in an hour."

"Mister Jackson, I got plenty of jugs if'n you mean drinkin' whiskey. No need to buy more."

Jackson then turned his attention to the rain-soaked young man whose head and hands were sticking through the stock. "Malcolm, Judge

McNairy has ordered you to be let out. If there is a next time of this type behavior I'll ask that you be publicly whipped, you understand?"

Malcolm Terrell did not answer. He glared at Jackson as he walked away massaging his chapped wrist.

An hour later, Andrew Jackson presented himself at Bob's door. After shaking the rain from his coat, he handed it to Bob who hung it on a nearby peg. Neither man knew how to proceed. A white man making a social call on a black man was a new experience for both.

"I believe you said you had a drink."

Bob threw back an animal skin to reveal a cache of jugs and selected one.

"You want a cup or you just drink from the jug? It ain't been touched."

Andrew Jackson could not believe what he had just seen. He picked up Bob's candle from the cask it sat on, held it aloft, and looked about the room. He saw food stores, tanned hides of several kinds of animals, and kegs stacked three deep and two high.

"Bob, this looks like a storeroom. What are you doing with all this merchandise?"

"You mean this stuff? I works for white people and they pays me. I help make whiskey all the time. Sometimes we do it on shares. I hunts, smoke meat, grind meal, whatever they wants, I do. I trade a little with the black folks. They ain't got much, but it don't hurt for them to have a few of the pleasures of life."

"You have so much here. Does your owner know about this?"

"Mistress Shaw ain't never been here. She say, 'Bob, you can keep what you earn.' This is what I earn."

"This is worth a lot of money."

"I don't have much need for money."

"I wish I could say that."

Andrew Jackson's astonishment at what he was seeing had made him forget his superior attitude. He thought, "This little black man has a small fortune in here, and nobody knows about it. And it's all his. Says he has no need of money, but I sure do." He blurted aloud, "Have you given consideration to employing an agent to act on your behalf."

"Mister Jackson, that must be lawyer talk, 'cause I ain't understood a word you say."

"Let me think about this for a minute." Jackson pulled the stopper from the jug and poured the clear liquid into a cup. He took the strong drink into his mouth and savored it briefly before swallowing it. He made the appropriate grimace and said, "That's good stuff" before pouring another. Then he remembered he was in this man's home, and his manners returned. Bob was no longer black; he was a potential client for the ambitious lawyer.

"Did you want a drink? I've been caught a little off guard and forgot myself."

"Oh, I drinks a little. I don't care much for that hot stuff. I like the more gen'le."

"What do you mean by more gentle?"

"I shows you."

89

Bob took a keg and pulled the plug. He picked up the lawyer's cup and tossed the contents in a nearby bucket. He poured two cups and handed one to Jackson. "I calls this sippin' whiskey."

A mellow taste sensation flooded Jackson's senses. His eyes got big, and he sipped again. "I've not tasted anything quite like this. You made this? How?"

"Well, suh, I don't rightly know. I think it got som'thin' to do with it bein' in the wood keg for a long time. And I do some things Ole Patsy told me works with cookin'."

Jackson mellowed a little after his second cup. "Bob, old boy, take my advice. Don't ever tell anyone how you produced this wonderful concoction. You have here a trade secret. Don't even tell your lawyer how you do it."

"That must be more lawyer talk."

"As a matter of fact, it is. But what you need now is an agent."

"What do a agent do?"

"He can turn all this into cash…for a small fee, of course."

They just sat there studying each other. Bob's normal demeanor was to have a smile on his face. Andrew Jackson was now grinning. He believed he had at last found a way to make money on the frontier. Bob would be his client, and he would be Bob's agent…for a small fee, of course.

"You say you have Mistress Shaw's permission to possess all of this. I must confirm that with her. Then we can go into business. You agree?"

"Mister Lawyer Jackson, I don't understand anything you have said in the last hour. Why did you want to see me today?"

"That's not important now. Listen closely, Bob. I will become your agent. We can take this room full of trade goods down the river and sell it for cash, gold. Or we can trade for goods that we can sell here. Do you understand?"

"You wants me to go down the river, with you and all my stuff. We gonna trade it for more stuff. Mister Jackson, Ole Black Bob do love to trade stuff for mo' stuff. If'n Mistress Shaw say I can leave Nashville, I'll go with you."

"Let me take care of that. I'll come back soon. Don't tell anyone about our contractual agreement. It will be just between us."

"Yes, suh, don't tell nobody Lawyer Jackson workin' for me."

Andrew Jackson paused just long enough to consider that a slave had just employed him. Then he considered the potential for profit and dismissed the thought.

The next morning, Andrew Jackson sought out Olive Shaw. He began by apologizing for not having called on her sooner. He had been so busy helping to establish the new court system he just didn't have the time. He knew, as a gentleman, he should have made the time. He told her that he had heard of her bravery on the trip to Nashville and all she had overcome to be the lady she was.

"From what I gather, it was you, Mrs. Crockrell, Mrs. Robertson, and Mrs. Donelson and other ladies that really made Nashville the place it is and will become."

"Oh, the men deserve some credit," she smiled. "Mister Jackson, why do I feel you want something from me?"

"Dear lady, you are too wise for me. In fact, I do want something. I would like to hire your man Bob to accompany me on a journey downriver. He has experience on flatboats. I need a man like Bob."

"Mister Jackson, surely you have heard about Nashville that Bob does as he pleases."

"Yes, I have heard that. But you see there are legal matters to be considered since we will leave the state and be gone for awhile. With your permission I will draw up the papers saying Bob is your property and you have authorized his traveling with me for the purpose of trading. Is there anything in Natchez I can bring back to you?"

"Mister Jackson, I'm sure a man as resourceful as yourself will find an appropriate bobble to thank a lady."

SEVEN
ANOTHER RIVER JOURNEY

General George Washington had been elected President of the United States of America. The capital of this loosely organized country was to be in Philadelphia. The citizens of Nashville received the news of the events of February 1789 with mixed feelings. Their main concerns with their new national government were land and slaves. North Carolina had an on-again, off-again willingness to cede its western lands. There was a land grab by politicians from the East. The land-grabbers then favored cession of the lands to the national government, provided existing claims were recognized. There also was an attempt to organize the western lands and enter the union as the State of Franklin, under the leadership of Colonel John Sevier. North Carolina had a change of heart and repealed the act of cession. The statehood movement then fell apart; however, the State of North Carolina was preparing once more to cede the lands to the federal government and adopt the new Constitution. The western lands of North Carolina would become a part of the Territory of the United States South of the River Ohio.

A concern to the citizens of Nashville was the Northwest Ordinances of 1787 that had set up a system whereby a territory with 60,000 inhabitants could apply for admission as a state with all the rights and privileges of the original thirteen. Of greater concern to Nashville was that the ordinances had abolished slavery in the Northwest Territories. The election of Washington, a slaveholder himself, calmed some of the fears.

Andrew Jackson, as a state official, had an interest in the political events, but his primary interest was in making his fortune. Jackson set about organizing the trading expedition for Bob and himself. Jackson had again been astonished when he mentioned to Bob that they needed to obtain a flatboat. "I knows how to build one," responded Bob. "I helped Mister Joseph and Mister Hodgson. I remembers it all." Bob did put one condition on his journey-to-be with Andrew Jackson: They would wait until spring. This time Bob did not have to cut the trees and saw the boards. Andrew Jackson went to the Richardson and Wallace Sawmill to arrange for all materials to be billed to his account. "Let Bob have whatever he wants, and I'll see that you get paid," he told Blake, the sawmill foreman, receiving another astonishment when he was told, "Mister Jackson, you don't need to vouch for Black Bob with me. I know his word is good."

Jackson assembled a work crew to build the boat. They were a mixed group of slaves and freemen. He made it clear to the freemen that they were working for him, not Black Bob. As the work progressed, a group of men stood watching the flurry of activity on the bank of the Cumberland River. They were watching Black Bob tactfully direct the building of the boat. One of them was Monsieur Timothy Demonbreun, the acknowledged first citizen of Nashville. He had come to the area as a fur trader over ten years before James Robertson. Out of respect, he was addressed by his French title. Monsieur Timothy observed, "It is not really a flatboat. It is what we

French call a *pirogue*. You notice the lines are much more graceful, better for moving through the water." All nodded agreement, bowing to the superior knowledge of the French-Canadian.

Andrew Jackson joined the men on the bank. The subject had turned from the craft to the builder. Andrew Holt said, "Mister Jackson, that is an unusual man you have working for you. He has boundless energy and seems to know exactly what he is doing. I would say he is a man with spizzerinctum."

Demonbreun cocked his head, "And what does that mean exactly, my learned friend?"

"Ah, yes. Well, it means he has a strong will to succeed, but it means more. It means he goes about it with a great deal of energy and enthusiasm. I think you would agree, it is a unique trait, and to find it in a black man in this day and time, the rarest of all."

Monsieur Timothy acknowledged, "You are most correct, sir. I have employed Bob many times. I have always found him to have, what you say, 'spizzerinctum.'"

Andrew Jackson and the bystanders nodded their agreement. Bob had overheard the conversation but pretended he was too busy with his work to be eavesdropping. He was pleased: "Just wait 'til I tells Ole Patsy I got spizzerinctum." He kept repeating the word over and over. The feel and the taste of the word satisfied a deep hunger within him.

II

"As soon as the spring session of court is over, we'll leave," said Jackson. "I have more than just your merchandise for us to carry. I could fill up two boats with the goods people want us to take and trade for them."

"For a small fee, of course," Bob response.

The cabin was smaller than the old *Paradise Bound's*. The cabin would be filled with goods that needed to be protected from the weather. This craft was to be a freight-hauler. It would not be sold for lumber at the end of the journey as a flatboat would. It would be sold as a first-rate boat. Bob mentioned that it could carry a sail if they wanted one. Jackson, knowing nothing about boats, decided the spring currents would be fast enough for him.

Lawyer Jackson had drawn up a cleverly conceived document that Olive Shaw gladly signed. It gave Bob permission to be in the company of Andrew Jackson for the purpose of trading goods and clearly stated that Bob could retain any money he made on said journey. The document would remain in effect until revoked by the consent of Andrew Jackson and/or Olive Shaw. He drew up a second document that he gave to Bob. It was folded carefully, wrapped in thin oilcloth, and stored in a pouch Bob was to carry around his neck at all times. This document plainly stated, "Any inquiry about said negro, Bob, should be addressed to A. Jackson, Esq."

"If you should have a problem, you tell whoever wants to know where they can find me. You won't be in Nashville where everybody knows you. Most of the people are our countrymen, but Natchez is under Spanish control. Remember your place."

"Yes, suh. I ain't ever been nowhere but here 'cept when I was a boy back East with the Renfros. I knows you'll look out for me…for a small fee, of course."

"Bob, I swear by the Eternal, sometimes you are too clever with words. But I suppose a lawyer should not complain about someone being clever with words."

"Yes, suh, it be hard for a man with spizzerinctum to keep his big mouth shut."

Jackson intended to have the last word. He intended to take charge here and now, but the glare from his dark blue eyes was met by the biggest grin he had ever seen. The whites of Bob's eyes and his teeth were highlighted through a black face with nothing but merriment on it.

"Bob, what will I ever do with you? I can't throw you overboard. You are too valuable. That's for sure."

Bob continued grinning, and a now satisfied Andrew Jackson had the last word. There was no discussion about naming their boat. Bob named it the *Small Fee,* but he did not share that with Andrew Jackson.

As they floated down the Cumberland, Bob kept up a running commentary instructing Jackson in handling the boat. When they came to the growing community of Clarksville located at the mouth of the Red River, Bob became reflective: "It was up that river where we lost Mister Joseph, Big Prometheus and so many more. It was a lot of people—men women and children—those red savages murdered. If'n we had kept the boat, we could have come out this way. They might be alive today." Jackson started to comment but then realized Bob was not talking to him. He decided he would leave Bob alone with his memories.

They floated as long as there was daylight and started again at first light. For nourishment, they chewed deer jerky. The third day, they made an early camp on the site where the greens had been gathered for "Miss Patsy's Salad." Bob began cooking for Andrew Jackson. They had not discussed cooking. They had just put together some food. Bob selected almost all of it and brought along an iron pot. What he ate did not make much difference to Jackson. Bob prepared two plates. Each had a large helping of the greens and a piece of fried ham with a corn cake. He handed one to Jackson and sat down on a log facing him. "Me and Young Mister William, he be Miss Olive's son, we use to hunt and be out like this. We had ourselves some times."

Since passing the Red River, Andrew Jackson had begun to reevaluate his traveling companion. He became aware that he had entered a new and private world. He had never even considered that this black man had a life; much less one that included the things he wished had been a part of own life. Jackson thought of his own orphaned childhood and the death of all those close to him. It had made him determined to make something out of himself. He would become wealthy and be a gentleman. Now he was with a man who found enjoyment in the simplest of life's pleasures, yet this was a man with a determination to succeed equal to his. Only their goals were different.

"Bob, this food is as good as I've ever had. Tell me again how it came to be discovered and how you hunted deer at night."

Bob again related the story of how Jack Civil had come up with the way of hunting deer at night. When he finished he said, "Mister Jackson I hears you kilt a panther with a tomahawk when you was comin' to Nashville."

"Who told you that?"

"That Annie girl you left at my place, God rest her soul."

"In fact, I did kill a big she-cat and her cub when they tried to get to the horses. I hear that your prowess as a hunter is legendary. Is there anything that you don't do, and do well?"

"To be truthful, Mister Jackson, I prob'ly the second best hunter in all of these parts. That be why we haulin' so many pelts and hides."

"How do you hunt bear? I've always heard about how dangerous bear hunting is."

"Huntin' bear is like cookin'— you can't be in no hurry. If'n you lets the dogs work, the bear will go up a tree. Then you just shoots 'em. That all there be to it. Folks that go to runnin' after a bear gonna end up fightin' that bear ever'time."

Jackson sat trying to figure out if Bob was pulling his leg. Finally he asked, "You said you were the second best hunter, who's the best?"

"Well, suh, I don't rightly know. If'n I said it be me, folks say I lyin' or boastin', so I just say I second best."

"Go to sleep." Jackson chuckled to himself admiring Bob's keen wit. If he had a flaw in his own character it was finding humor and enjoying it at his own expense.

The next day they floated down the Ohio River, traveling in two hours what it had taken the Donelson Party eight days to cover going upstream. As they passed the Tennessee, Bob shouted back, "That be one river I didn't much care if'n I ever saw again. We almost meet our Maker on it. We near froze, had the pox, fought murderin' redskins, ran fast water, almost run out of food. Ever'thin' that could go wrong went wrong. Miss Olive, she say the Lord was movin' in mysterious ways. He sho' 'nuff was."

Bob had come close enough to a subject Andrew Jackson wanted to talk about.

"That was where you saved the life of Mistress Rachel Robards, was it not?"

"Oh, I just gave her a hand gettin' out of the water."

"That is not the way she tells it. I'd like to hear more about it."

Bob had no trouble translating that statement to mean he wanted to hear more about young Rachel. The image of her spearing fish came to his mind as he remembered thinking, "That girl gonna cause some man a lot of trouble." And then he thought of the storm he believed would follow this man. Now they had met. "Lordy, Lordy, Lordy," was all Bob could utter to himself.

When they came in sight of the Mississippi River neither was prepared for the awesome sight before them. Water spread out for miles. Moving into the mainstream was like going down hill. It was not as fast as

Bob remembered Muscle Shoals. There appeared to be no dangerous rocks. There were sandbars in the bends, but their small craft in midstream was handling beautifully. Jackson had become proficient on the tiller and enjoyed the exhilaration of rapid movement. Jackson had experienced something similar on horseback, but a horse could not sustain this pace for very long. As the sun set, he picked a campsite near a small creek.

"You want fish or rabbit?" asked Bob.

"You've got fish?"

"Oh, no, suh, but this stream do."

Later, after they had eaten their fill of fish, Jackson again brought the conversation around to Rachel. Bob related the story of the youngsters providing everyone with fish to eat and Captain Donelson not considering it to be real meat.

"He could be hardheaded. Now you take Miss Rachel, that girl could get more fish than all them boys put together. She had her a forked spear. She kept the points sharp, and her aim was steady and true. When she jabbed the water, a fish came out."

Andrew Jackson smiled at the image. His smile grew wider when he repeated Bob's words to himself, "Now you take Miss Rachel." He would like to…but Miss Rachel was a married woman. He went to sleep hoping to continue the dream.

Bob looked at the man smiling in his sleep. "Lordy, Lordy, trouble be a comin'."

The next day they started to see small settlements along the river, and then they arrived at Natchez. Andrew Jackson was a whirlwind trading their goods. Within hours, he and Bob were dressed in new clothes. He consulted Bob about the things he might want purchased for their return trip. He did not feel the need to use Bob's trading skills. For his part, Bob stayed out of the way. He was uncomfortable around so many strange people, and he was even more uncomfortable when, for the first time, he saw a slave market with black people in chains. Men, women, and children were being sold. Some were sold outright; others went on auction. Andrew Jackson looked over the slaves but did not purchase. He didn't want the problems of transporting them back to Nashville, and he had lost money when Annie died. Jackson seemed oblivious to the fact that Bob was a slave, and it was Bob's fortune that he was trading.

Bob was left behind while Andrew Jackson went with several gentlemen for an evening of drinking and pleasure. Bob was wandering about when night fell. A burly white man walked toward him with purpose. When he was about six feet away he spoke loudly, "You there, darkie, stop!"

Bob came to an immediate stop.

The man spoke again, "What do you think you are doing out at night without your master? You are violating the law."

Bob had long ago developed the habit of speaking in the dialect that suited his purpose. Taking his old friend Prometheus's advice, he had developed his own combination of words. Most often he spoke in a dialect that could only be described as somewhere between an ignorant African and an educated white man. There was seldom a problem with making himself understood to anyone. He had been around educated white people all of his life, and he knew the language well. It was time to use it.

"Sir, are you addressing me? I assure you that I am here with the full knowledge of Lawyer Andrew Jackson in whose company I am traveling."

The deputy sheriff was taken aback. "I am talking to you. Where you from?"

"Sir, I arrived only recently. We traveled down river from Nashville. We are trading our goods and will return soon."

"Where is this Jackson fellow?"

"He left in the company of several prominent local gentlemen. I should think you would find him in your finest dining establishment."

The deputy had hoped to intimidate Bob. Now he felt on the defensive. This well-dressed black man was obviously one of those potentates he had heard about, and he looked for a way to exit this conversation.

"Well, you better get off the streets. It's not safe out alone at night."

"I shall take your advice. A good evening to you, sir."

Bob made his way to where they had docked the boat. Once alone, out of sight from the rest of the world, he doubled up with laughter.

The next morning Andrew Jackson happened to mention that he had lost a great deal gambling. He had enough to pay the people back in Nashville their due, but his fees and Bob's money were gone. Jackson reasoned that a black man, still a slave, had little need of money. True, he had gambled away Bob's money, but it was money he should not have had in the first place. His mistress should have kept better track of him. That reasoning made it Olive

Shaw's money he had lost. Then Jackson went back to having lost Bob's money. He knew that he was indebted to his black traveling companion. His only explanation was that he had made a slight miscalculation.

"Well, suh, we still got the boat to trade. All that other stuff was gettin' in my way anyhow. I can get more. We had us a good time. I got me some fine new clothes. Let's go home," Bob said calmly. He truly meant it. He felt badly for his lawyer-agent. The fortune the lawyer was hoping for was now gone. They began to gather their rifles, clothing, and Bob's cooking equipment.

"Bob, what is this keg with candle wax on it?"

"That be the keg I kept my candle on. It got whiskey in it. Matter-of-fact, we ought to have a drink right now. It make you feel better."

They took out their cups, propped up the keg, and pulled the cork. After his first sip, Andrew Jackson leaped to his feet. "By the Eternal, Bob, this is the best yet. Put that cork back in. This is too good for one man to possess it all. I have an idea."

Andrew Jackson found a table nearby and set up a concession. He guaranteed, for a small fee, the best whiskey ever tasted. Word spread. Within hours Bob was draining the last drops from the keg, and Andrew Jackson was promising every whiskey dealer in Natchez that he would bring more soon.

They traded the boat. Bob had explained to the purchaser that this boat would sail as well as any he had ever seen, and with a little practice he could make it sail upstream. The value of the boat increased. They left Natchez astride two fine mounts, each of them leading two packhorses loaded with merchandise. When they arrived at their campsite, Bob spoke, "Mister Jackson, you ain't gonna be able to deliver on that whiskey promise you made."

"What do you mean? You can make more."

"Not like that I can't. I been studyin' on it. I ain't got the first notion of how it was made. I poured different jugs into that keg, made by different people I helped, and it been sittin' in my place for years."

"You think on it some more, Bob. I'll bet you can come close."

"Yes, suh, but ain't you had enough of bettin'?"

III

During the overland journey to Nashville, Andrew Jackson experienced more of Bob's creativeness with a cooking pot. They dined on small game and fowl. Often they were able to spot and hunt the game as they rode. They usually ate long after dark because of Bob's insistence that good cooking could not be rushed. Every third day they had a stew made from the leftovers.

Upon their arrival in Nashville, Jackson and Bob, dressed in his new clothes, called upon Olive Shaw. Their intent was to deliver a small box containing three pairs of lace gloves in different colors. Olive Shaw was dressed in black. She informed them that word had been sent to her from Virginia that her beloved son William had died of a fever. Bob felt the loss of his dearest male companion, the man who was his would-be blood brother.

Andrew Jackson carried a similar box of gloves to the Widow Donelson, while Bob presented Patsy with a colorful bandana and a small sack containing seeds for growing okra. Patsy and Bob swapped stories.

"Miss Rachel done told her ma she is powerful unhappy. She afraid dat man she married gonna kill her."

"He do, and Mister Jackson kill him 'fore the sun sets," Bob declared. "I believe he do it if she just harmed. Mister Jackson asked me 'bout her ever' day. He want to know ever' thing 'bout her."

"Lordy, what we gonna do? She a married woman, and Mister Jackson got the fever for her. It gonna be worse 'fore it get better."

Bob nodded his agreement and added, "That Mister Jackson got enough spizzerinctum for ten men. He gonna be important one of these days."

"You and dat Mister Lawyer Andrew Jackson can just take yo spizz someplace else, 'cause I ain't got time for yo nonsense."

Andrew Jackson purchased a still and all the supplies Bob told him would be needed for the manufacturing of whiskey. Jackson told Bob there was no need to hunt for hides and pelts. "Whiskey is where the money is. You just brew up your magic elixir. That is all we will take on our next trip." Jackson even arranged for kegs and firewood to be delivered to the still. Bob experimented. He added a little of this and a little of that until he believed he had a good mixture that aging in wooden kegs would only improve. Jackson arranged for the discarded mixtures to be sold. Bob's reputation as a cook and whiskey-maker was growing so much that his discarded batches were considered better than most. Jackson also commanded Bob to put a sail on the new boat. "We'll want to travel as fast as possible," he said, "and I have it on good authority that a boat with sail will bring a higher price a little farther downriver in New Orleans."

Bob busied himself with the task Jackson set out for him. He now had an experienced boat building crew, and the mash for whiskey needed time to work. He had time to attend to other concerns. There were still frequent Indian attacks around Nashville. He accompanied parties of men hunting down marauding Indians. These militia groups valued Bob's skill as a tracker and stalker. After the Indians were driven out and property recovered, Bob's skill with the cookfire was even more appreciated.

Patsy informed him that things were getting worse. Miss Rachel was coming home again, and Andrew Jackson was moving out of the Donelson household. He was moving to nearby Mansker Station. "Dat sho ain't far 'nough away. Dey's gonna be a killing for sure. Miss Rachel can control that fool lawyer a little bit, but dat man just plain crazy when it come to dat girl," Patsy declared.

"Our boat's almost ready. We ain't got all the whiskey he want. As soon as we do, maybe he leave for awhile."

Bob's words seemed prophetic when Andrew Jackson gave him his orders, "Bob, load the boat with what we have. Don't put anything in the cabin. We're going to join a group leaving in two days. When you get it loaded, take the boat to the Widow Donelson's. I'll meet you there."

"Yes, suh. What 'bout Mistress Shaw? She say I can go?"

"Our agreement is still in effect. Nothing to concern yourself with."

Two days later, Bob had a half-full boat docked on the shore near the Donelson home. Servants carried trunks to the boat under the watchful eye of Andrew Jackson. Bob desperately wanted to see Patsy and ask her about the things he was witnessing, but the opportunity did not present itself. Jackson appeared on the bank accompanied by Rachel.

She spoke to Bob, "I hope I will not be as much trouble as on our last voyage."

"Missy, you goin' with us? To Natchez?"

Jackson interrupted, "Mistress Robards will accompany us. We will transport her to the safety of friends near Natchez. Join up with Colonel Stark's boats when they come by. We will travel in their company."

The trip to Natchez was uneventful. There was no need of a sail. The Stark party consisted of several flatboats with full loads. Jackson and Rachel spent most of the daylight hours talking. At night Rachel slept in the boat's cabin with Jackson standing guard. Jackson was determined that everyone was aware that Mistress Robard's honor was not being compromised. Bob found very little time to talk with either of them. Shortly after their arrival, Jackson departed with Rachel. Within the hour he returned, informing Bob they would continue down to New Orleans. Shortly after they departed Bob grew fearful, for he had noticed that the riverbank was teeming with huge monsters. He pointed them out to Mister Jackson who calmed him by saying they were local scavengers called alligators. A look at the long, tooth-filled mouth convinced Bob that this was no place to be in the water. "Miss Olive know for sure this be the gate to hell, and it be guarded by these ugly beasts."

Andrew Jackson spent little time at trading. He took the first reasonable offer for the whole load and then traded the boat. Bob was able to make a couple of trades on his own. The following morning they departed in the direction of Natchez, each was riding a horse with Bob leading their lone pack animal. Bob also had a banjo on his back. From time to time, he would draw the instrument forward and try to pick a tune. The man he had traded with showed him how to strum it and informed him that by moving his fingers he could make different sounds. Jackson did not seem to

109

be bothered by his attempts at making music. As a matter-of-fact, nothing bothered Andrew Jackson. He was too preoccupied.

They stopped only briefly in Natchez and were off again. They were cautioned that the trail to Nashville had recently had an outbreak of criminal activity. Jackson assured everyone that he was well armed and any highwaymen he didn't kill, he would see hanged. He meant for the word to be spread among those planning on following him out of Natchez with an intent to rob him that it would be their last criminal act.

Jackson was not in a mood for enjoying Bob's company, food, or music.

"Bob, stop torturing that infernal instrument," he blared.

"Yes, suh." After a brief pause, he spoke, "Mister Jackson, Miss Rachel gonna stay down here perm'nent? She ain't gonna go back to the Cumberland?"

Jackson had no intention of explaining anything until he recalled Bob's long acquaintance with Rachel. "These are difficult times. In my opinion, she was in great danger in Nashville. I think she will be safe in Natchez."

They sat in silence for awhile before Jackson began thinking out loud, "I'll need to make money. To my way of thinking, there are three ways: land, whiskey, and slaves."

"Mister Jackson, I can help with the whiskey. I ain't allowed to own land, and for sure I ain't yo' man to help with no slaves."

Jackson sensed Bob's uneasiness about slavery. He offered an explanation: "You are one in a million, Bob, maybe one in ten million. You are the only slave I ever saw who can take care of himself."

"No, suh. Lots of black people do al'right if just left alone. They just ain't got the chance. I don't know many black people. Mo' and mo' being brought to Nashville. Won't be long they be runnin' away. They don't even know where they runnin' to. They just be goin'.'"

Andrew Jackson took on the role of teacher. He was going to convince the man before him that it was the natural order of things for Africans to be slaves. "That's what I mean. They need someone to look after them. You see, they are captured by their own countrymen and sold to slavers. In Africa, they are naked savages. Some are cannibals. When they are put on ships, they are being shipped to a new life where they will be fed and clothed in return for their labor."

"Mister Jackson, in all respect, I don't know nothin' about Africa. I just know this country. I have seen some people brought here from Africa. I seen some in Natchez and New Orleans. They don't act happy to be here."

"They will be. They are ignorant. It will take a little time for them to learn. They will soon see that it is God's will. Some are meant to be masters, others slaves."

"Is that what be in your Bible? Miss Rachel use to read it to me some."

"Well, yes, it is in the Bible. I know Miss Rachel wants you to be free. She told me we need to make new laws. What is more important is that slaves are part of an economic system that supports the growth of our new country."

"Yes, suh, I hear'd 'bout the new country. I hear'd it say that all men be created free and equal."

"Bob, your logic is not correct. It means all white men are free and equal. What you are referring to was written by white men for white men. Most of them are slaveholders themselves."

"Mister Jackson, as near as I can figure, white men just take what they wants. They takes the land from the red men and puts black men to work on it and calls it theirs and say it's in the Bible that way."

Andrew Jackson knew that he would have to take another approach with Bob. He tried again: "You have been given a little freedom and prospered. You surely don't believe there are others among your race who could do the same? You are what is known as 'the exception that proves the rule.'"

"Mister Jackson, I do believe you are talkin' lawyer talk again 'cause I don't understand. White folks say it all 'cause it be God's will. Ain't he the God of black folks too? Don't 'set my people free' mean us too?"

Jackson was perplexed. He needed time to think. He was a lawyer, not a theologian. Bob's arguments were not what he had expected. He did not want to consider any validity in what Bob said. His future depended on the status quo. Slavery was a valid step in his road to riches.

"We'll talk more on this another time. We need an early start tomorrow. I want to get back to Nashville as soon as possible."

After their return to Nashville, Bob saw little of Andrew Jackson. It was not mentioned as to whether he should start stockpiling for another journey, so Bob returned to his old life. He helped all who wanted assistance at whatever they wanted. He had possession of the still Jackson had purchased. During slack times, he brewed up batches of whiskey. He enjoyed the experimentation just as he enjoyed mixing soups and stews. As in the past, he went often to talk with Patsy. She was his source for news. "I hears your Mistress near goin' out of her mind with grief," Patsy reported. "She gittin' old, and she just done lost too much. She act a little crazy som'time."

Bob felt the need to defend Miss Olive. "She be all right. She been through a lot, but she get over it and be strong again. I remember when Mister Joseph was kilt. She tried to warn Mister Jones, but he don't listen. She didn't just sit 'round waitin', we left. They all got kilt. She just took over ever'thing, and we all survived. She a strong woman."

"She a old woman. That make a difference."

They dropped the subject. "You plant that okra I brung you?"

"Sho 'nuff. I fix it all kind of ways. Put some cornmeal batter on it. Fry it, boil it, mix it in soup. It don't look like much, but it good."

Their visits went predictably through the summer months until August, when Patsy asked Bob, "You didn't go with 'em dis time?"

"What you talkin' 'bout, woman?"

"Mister Jackson. He done gone to see Miss Rachel. He told Ole Miss Rachel he gonna marry her."

Bob showed his surprise, "He didn't say nothin' to me 'bout goin'. Her husband dead?"

"No. Som'thin' to do with de law. Say they ain't married no more."

"Oh, Lordy. Miss Rachel and Mister Andrew married to each other. I guess we just wait 'n see what storms are a comin'."

A group of ladies called on Mistress Olive Shaw. They felt it was their Christian duty to comfort the aging woman. It was rumored she was becoming senile and forgetful. As with most gatherings these days, the gossip turned to Andrew and Rachel Jackson.

"And the divorce is not final. They are not married. They are living in sin," Christine Dean preached.

"That Robards tricked them," added Carol Reeves. "He let it be known that he was divorcing Rachel, then didn't follow through with it. Olive, you have known the Donelsons a long time; what do you think?"

Olive gathered her facilities and responded, "She was always a headstrong girl, doing as she pleased and no one to correct her. She was the youngest, you know."

Mistress Dean responded, "Well, any way you say it, the fact remains that that Rachel Donelson is now a bigamist. Married to two men at the same time. And if your man hadn't helped him, he couldn't have done it."

Olive rose to the bait, "Just what does that mean, my man helped?"

"Your man, the one they call Black Bob, went with Mister Jackson trading all of that whiskey. Then he helped Mister Jackson secret her off to Natchez. He even built the boats for Mister Jackson."

"Bob had my permission to travel with Mister Jackson. Mister Jackson asked for his help, and I agreed."

"They must have tricked you, bless your heart. How could you know what they were plotting," Mistress Dean said in her most sympathetic tone.

Olive Shaw began to feel that accusations were being leveled at her. Long after her guests departed, she was convincing herself that she must do something to right this wrong and convince the ladies of Nashville that she had no hand in this tawdry affair. Had Bob really abetted Andrew Jackson in the elopement? She never gave permission for Jackson to use him as a way of seducing Rachel, or was it the other way around? Through Bob, she had become involved. She was an accomplice. She had to find a way out.

Several days passed before Olive came to a solution. Word passed rapidly down the banks of the Cumberland to the Donelson farm. Patsy delivered the news to Rachel Jackson.

"Andrew! Andrew!" screamed Rachel.

Andrew Jackson was at Rachel's side in an instant, "What has alarmed you so, my love?"

"Patsy just told me. Olive Shaw has sold Bob!"

EIGHT
SOLD INTO SLAVERY – 1792

Olive Shaw had sold Bob to John Mays. Mays owned a number of slaves and was often involved in purchase and sell transactions. Bennett Searcy, who had come to Nashville with Jackson, was the lawyer who drew up the legal papers.

"Bennett, what happened with Olive Shaw?" quizzed a distraught Andrew Jackson. "I would have purchased Bob myself if I had known she was willing to sell him."

"Calm down, old friend, I'm just handling the legal work. The deal was struck before I was sent for. I'm not at liberty to discuss Mistress Shaw's business affairs. I can tell you this—she would not have sold him to you under any circumstances."

Jackson knew not to press for answers to the questions he most wanted answered. "What does John Mays want with Bob? Bob is not a field hand. He's a jack-of-all-trades, but he cannot read and write. At least, not well enough to keep books. Though he does have a remarkable memory. Still, he cannot write it down. I just cannot imagine what Mays wants him for. Maybe he will resell him," Jackson said, trying to come up with an explanation for Rachel.

"Andrew, we've fought Indians, and we've worked together. We've been friends for a long time. Take my advice. Do not get involved in this now. You cannot change it. You might talk with my brother about your options."

Bennett Searcy could not tell Andrew Jackson that one of the stipulations made by Olive Shaw was that under no circumstances was Jackson to come into ownership of Bob. It would never appear in a legal document, but the pledge was just as strong. The only way for Bennett to help his friend was through his brother Robert who was an attorney with a wide range of business interests.

Robert Searcy, as did all of Nashville, knew and liked Bob. He told Jackson, "I'll keep a watch on the situation, and if the opportunity arises, I'll do whatever I can. Opportunity and timing are the keys to success in this type of venture. We must bide our time and move at just the right moment."

Bob was stunned. It came back to him what the slave men had told him years before that he "was property to be sold like a horse." He didn't hold malice toward Mistress Shaw. "She just a po' old woman who done lost her husband and now her son. She sick with grief. She don't know what she doin' half the time. Maybe she get better and buy me back."

John Mays did not know what he was going to do with Bob. He had observed Bob at work and thought he would make a good overseer. But, he had not made allowance for the melancholy mood that would settle over Bob, nor had he given thought that Bob had little experience interacting with other slaves. Mays was also disturbed by a rumor that had recently come his way. He wasn't sure of its source; some attributed it to the Searcy brothers. The rumor was that Mays would be best advised not to mix Bob in with his fieldhands. Bob had some peculiar ideas on the institution of slavery. He had been conditioned by his circumstances to think like a freeman. Such a man mixed in with ignorant slaves could infect the whole lot's thinking. A slave insurrection was a possibility. Mays also did not like the fact that so many influential men were concerned about the welfare of this slave. He decided to sell Bob at the first opportunity. He sold Bob to a Nashville attorney, Josiah Love.

Josiah Love's ownership of Bob was brief and filled will legal maneuvering. For almost two years Bob was in a legal limbo. Love was indebted to Robert Nelson. In April 1793, Nelson recovered a judgment against Love. None other than Andrew Jackson represented Love in court. To satisfy the judgment, Nelson claimed Bob. On the day Nelson intended to sell Bob, Love obtained an injunction to stop the sale. Love then entered a complicated arrangement with Elijah Robertson, the brother of James Robertson, in which Love sold Bob to Robertson and in return received the loan of another slave named Jim. The Davidson County Court of Equity dissolved the injunction bill of Josiah Love vs. Robert Nelson and ordered the Clerk of Davidson County to sell Love's property to satisfy his debt. The only known property belonging to Love was Bob. When the sheriff conducted the sale, the highest bidder was one Robert Searcy, Esq.

Bob's woes were not over. Elijah Robertson claimed ownership also. Searcy and Robertson agreed to let the Superior Court of North Carolina, Mero District, decide ownership. In the meantime they agreed that Bob should pursue an activity for which he was well suited. On January 16, 1794, the County Court of Davidson County recorded in its minutes:

Bob Permitted To Sell Liquor

On motion made, the Court agrees that a certain Negro in the Town
Of Nashville, called Bobb, be permitted to sell Liquor and Victuals
On his Good Behavior, until the end of the next ensuing County Court.

Bob went into business. He opened an establishment that would be known forever as *Black Bob's Tavern*.

The case before the Superior Court became even more complex when Elijah Robertson died. But finally, in November 1795, judges John McNairy and Joseph Anderson handed down their decision:

Judgement of the Court:

After mature consideration it is the opinion of the Court: as the Sheriff had began to make Execution before the injunction was delivered to him that the venditoni Exponas issued from the County Court of Davidson ordered by the said Court of Equity was well awarded and legally served on said Negro Bob & Robert Searcy being the Purchaser under said Execution thereby obtained the legal right to said Negro.

"Well, Bob," Robert Searcy, who was enjoying a drink in *Black Bob's Tavern*, started, "you have become quite a celebrity. Our highest court decided your fate. Now here is what I expect. You will continue to operate this business. I have it on the highest authority that you are both intelligent and industrious."

Bob interrupted, "Yes, suh, my spizzerinctum has come back to me."

"To continue," said Searcy, after a sideways glance at Bob, "I expect you to return a profit on my investment. I am, however, a reasonable man. When my investment in you has been repaid, I will consider emancipating you."

"What do 'emancipating' mean?" asked Bob

"Why to emancipate is to set free. You will be a freeman with all the rights and privileges granted thereto."

"Mister Searcy, being a freeman is what I wants most. I will work hard for both of us." After a long pause Bob added, "I do like the way you lawyers talk. I just wish I understand you better."

"My dear fellow, if you understood, there would be no point to having lawyers."

II

Other than the court case involving Bob, only one other topic merited discussion in *Black Bob's Tavern*: statehood. Vermont and Kentucky had joined the United States. The flag of the United States of America now had fifteen stars and fifteen stripes. There were more than seventy thousand inhabitants in the Territory South of the River Ohio, and those in the East, those who had wanted the State of Franklin, favored statehood. Andrew Jackson had suggested that they adopt the name Tennessee. He had seen the early maps of General Daniel Smith in which Smith had labeled the area "Tennessee Territory," possibly a reference to an Indian tribe or their chief. Jackson liked the sound of the word. The county formed along the Red River also bore the name "Tennessee."

Several learned men had gathered at Bob's place to debate their positions. They had started coming to Bob's when they were students at the Davidson Academy. Bob's was their place, the place where they knew their friends would be and intellectual conversation stimulated

"What about the tax they put on whiskey?" argued David Lamb. "George Washington sent an army of over thirteen thousand into Pennsylvania to collect his taxes. Old Bob here will be one of the biggest taxpayers in the country. We've got local tax, state tax, and national tax on whiskey. It seems to me we are just asking for more taxes. What did we fight the war for?"

"We fought the war to have a say in the taxation," was Charles Waters' contribution to the discussion. "Taxation without representation, you'll recall. If we join the Union, we will have our representation."

"I'm not so sure," posed Preston Hubbard. "It appears to me that George Washington is setting himself up to be king."

"You're wrong there, Preston. The Constitution keeps that from happening," said Paul Hyatt. "Besides, Washington has no bloodline descendents to inherit his throne."

They all appreciated the spirit and humor of the debates. In *Black Bob's Tavern* the debate took on the character of the proprietor. Bob's demeanor was always pleasant, and Bob had developed his own method of keeping the liquor flowing at a level to stimulate conversation, but not enough to develop the brawls that were occurring elsewhere. It was just good business. No gentleman wanted to frequent a business where he had to be concerned for his safety. Most of the regulars knew that when Bob was pressed, his main concern was whether or not the new state would have a way for him to achieve the freedom that had been promised him.

"For the time being that is in the hands of the states," Hubbard informed him. "Our new state would have the say-so for the next twenty years."

"True enough," said Hyatt, "but, there are going to be more and more slaves." The big farmers believe it to be their best source of cheap labor."

Waters added, "The New England ship owners have been, and still are, the source of slaves. Now their states want to change the system. They take the profit, and then act sanctimonious."

David Lamb, announcing his intention to call it a night, concluded the debate for this evening: "So the question is, 'Do we join a flawed system and work to improve it or continue with the system we have developed here on the frontier?' It suits our current purpose, but cannot endure much longer. Gentlemen, we are no longer isolated."

The vote in Davidson County was ninety-six for statehood and five hundred seventeen opposed. The heavily populated eastern counties, however, had voted in overwhelming numbers to join the Union. *Black Bob's Tavern* in Nashville, Tennessee, was not the only place where the admission of the aspiring state was debated. In Philadelphia, the Halls of Congress saw much division, particularly in the Senate. A presidential election was coming up. President Washington had announced his intention to retire to Mount Vernon. The balance of power was at stake. On the last day of the legislative session, the Congress agreed to admit Tennessee. On June 1, 1796, George Washington signed the documents admitting Tennessee as the sixteenth state. Andrew Jackson, who had been a delegate to the Tennessee Constitutional Convention, was elected Tennessee's first congressman. William Cocke and William Blount were to be Tennessee's first senators, and John Sevier was elected governor.

Bob was pleased with the results of the election. He looked forward to the day he could vote. There were 3,613 people over sixteen years of age in Davidson County. Only six of them were free people of color, and only males could vote. Bob was numbered among the 992 slaves. According to Andrew Jackson, the Tennessee Constitution did not specifically address slavery. His legal opinion was that the procedures of North Carolina would probably be followed unless the legislative branch decided otherwise. Bob recalled that Miss Olive had told him new laws would be needed. "No laws" did not mean "new laws." But, he had years before he needed to be concerned with the laws of emancipation.

NINE
EMANCIPATION

Life in the new state of Tennessee was good for Andrew Jackson. After one year in the House of Representatives, the Tennessee General Assembly elected Jackson a United States senator. In September 1779, Governor John Sevier gave him an interim appointment to the Superior Court of Law and Equity. The General Assembly made the appointment permanent in December of that same year, when they selected Jackson over Bennett Searcy.

Life was good for Bob too. *Black Bob's Tavern* was a success, and Bob soon put aside most of the money to purchase his freedom. No one, however, seemed to be in any hurry to attend to the legal business necessary to accomplish emancipation. Many jurisdictional matters of more importance were still to be decided in the fledgling state. Most people treated Bob as a freeman and gave it little thought until an event happened in April 1800 that focused attention on Bob and his status. Bob was physically assaulted.

When Bob was out of hearing distance, Paul Hyatt reported to David Lamb that an eye-witness had told him that Bob was having a civil conversation with Schoolmaster Anderson Lavender as they stood outside watching the construction of a new log building. Bob apparently decided to impress the schoolmaster with his own mastery of the English language and began to speak and structure his sentences very much like Lavender's speech. Lavender took it to be mockery of himself and his exalted position. He suddenly picked up a sharp tool used for rough-shaping wood and threatened to "split your head open and remove your heathen tongue." As word got around the small community, the story was embellished to be a near murder. The incident seemed to take on a life of its own. Most citizens were sympathetic to Bob's plight. Charles Waters summed it all up: "Just because the schoolmaster thought a negro had forgotten his manners and appeared uppity was no reason to try to kill him. Besides we're talking about Black Bob, and everyone knows he is a genteel soul. Bob was being a little playful perhaps, but meant no harm. Schoolmasters shouldn't be imbibing in the middle of the day anyway."

Without giving any thought to the legal problems they were about to cause, the Grand Jury of Davidson County issued an indictment of Anderson Lavender.

Anderson Lavender late of the County of Davidson, Schoolmaster, on the twenty-fifth day of April in the year of our Lord one thousand eight hundred, with force and arms at the County of Davidson aforesaid in the town of Nashville, with a certain foot-adze which the sd. Anderson then and there held in his right hand, in and upon one black Negro man named Bob in the peace of God and our State then and there being did make an assault and battery with an intent him the said Bob then and there feloniously, willfully and of his malice aforethought to kill & murder, against the Statue in such case made and provided, and against the peace and dignity of our State.

John C. Hamilton Attor.
For the State

Legal minds began to ponder uneasily. Bennett Searcy privately quizzed his brother: "What in heaven's name have we done? A white freeman has been indicted for attacking a slave." There was no easy way out because it had been entered in the official records, and John Hamilton had no intention of admitting to a legal faux pas.

This was one subject that was not fully discussed inside *Black Bob's Tavern* except to assure Bob that nothing would happen to him. But, it was discussed at every other gathering of men in Nashville. Although Robert Searcy agreed that the indictment should have mentioned Bob was his property, he did not push the issue "What's done is done," he opined. "Let's just let it run its course."

Judge Andrew Jackson had some soul searching to do. He and his colleagues Archibald Roane and David Campbell worried about the legal precedent that would be established if a white man was found guilty of assaulting a slave. They weren't even sure if their court had jurisdiction. In the end they agreed with Robert Searcy, took the case, and let a jury hear the evidence.

Anderson Lavender's attorney entered a plea of "not guilty." The jury had a difficult time. In private they agreed not to agree and returned to an anxious court to announce their non-decision. The solution then became simple—just dismiss the case. The .attorney for the state announced he would seek no further prosecution of the indictment if Lavender would pay the cost of the prosecution. All parties agreed.

On the advice of Robert Searcy, Bob had said nothing during the hearing nor was he asked to testify. Bob enjoyed the proceedings immensely.

He liked being the center of attention, and he liked to hear the lawyers talk. He gave some thought that if ever he was a freeman, he might become a lawyer. He chuckled to himself, "Talking like a lawyer got me in this predicament…now I thinking about being one. I best stick to operating a tavern."

Unlike Bob, Andrew Jackson was troubled by the proceedings. He confessed to Rachel, "I'm not sure what we have done. I do know that we have afforded to Bob a status not granted to any other slave. Personally, none of us consider him a slave, yet legally he is Searcy's property. I don't see how, again legally, we can say he only has half-status. God help us if some ambitious attorney brings suit on behalf of a slave using this case as precedent."

Rachel saw her long-awaited opportunity: "The solution is so simple, my love. Just free Bob!" she shouted with glee. "Grant him all the rights of a freeman. God and man know he deserves his total freedom. So you men got the cart before the horse; it'll make no difference to anyone in Nashville."

"Rachel, you are trying to be Solomon; but, on further consideration, you do display a certain wisdom. The timing couldn't be better. We are about to elect a new governor, one that is familiar with this case. It'll take some careful political maneuvering," he mused. "We must carefully plant this seed in the minds of the men of Nashville."

II

On September 23, 1801, Judge Andrew Jackson administered the oath of office for the Office of Governor to his fellow judge and friend Archibald Roane. By this time Bob had accumulated the capital to purchase his freedom. In fact, he had accumulated much more, but purchasing one's freedom and obtaining one's freedom were separate and complicated issues. Robert Searcy acknowledged to all that Black Bob had been one of the most successful investments he had made. Searcy further acknowledged that, in fact, he had agreed that if Bob prospered and made a profit he would be allowed to purchase himself. Robert Searcy, Esq. was also a man who knew his way around the laws of Tennessee. He had spent time in Knoxville as the General Assembly's treasurer, so he was aware that the First General Assembly had emancipated a slave named "Jack" at the request of John Stone

Bob, for his part, had continued to ingratiate himself to the leading citizens of Nashville. They all knew that Bob ran an orderly house. He prepared the best food and served the best spirits. He occasionally plucked out a self-styled tune on his banjo. He knew when to add to a conversation and when to keep his mouth shut. He was a man to be trusted, for he knew many of their secrets but did not discuss them with others. Once it was known that Robert Searcy was willing to set Bob free, this became the main topic of conversation in the tavern. Richard Cross, a prominent merchant who also operated a private house of entertainment for gentlemen boarders, and

Benjamin J. Bradford, the publisher of the *Tennessee Gazette*, took leading roles. A handwritten petition addressed to the Fourth General Assembly of the State of Tennessee that would soon begin in Knoxville was drafted:

To the honorables the General Assembly of the State of Tennessee

The petition of Sundry the inhabitants of Davidson County Sheweth that a negro man called Bob, who now is and has for a number of years been an inhabitant of Davidson C., the town of Nashville, has by his industry and economy raised money & purchased himself but cannot enjoy that freedom which through his labour and perseverance he has become intitled too unless by act of the General Assembly.

Your petitioners therefore hope you will by act of your honorable body emancipate said negro, Bob. Giving him all the privileges that is usually to persons in a similar situation and your petitioners will ever pray.

Richard Cross had prepared the petition and was the first to sign. B.J. Bradford was next. Fifty-one more of the most distinguished white male citizens of Nashville signed the petition, four of whom were future mayors of the city. Among the signers was William Lytle, Jr., a member of the Lavender jury. Others included J.B. Craighead, attorney-merchant and son of the Presbyterian minister; Thomas Mallory, the surveyor of Nashville and signer of the 1780 Cumberland Compact; Joseph Elliston, silversmith; John Parker, tavern owner; Judge John McNairy, Sheriff J. H. Boyd, and Robert Searcy.

Bradford and Searcy discussed strategy.

"We can expect some assistance from my brother Free Masons," Searcy confided. "We are well organized throughout the state now."

"We'll have no problem in the Governor's Office," Bradford said. "Judge Jackson will see to that."

"I am willing to draft the legislation," Searcy said. "I have another issue on which I wish the General Assembly to give me favorable consideration."

"Another issue? It won't harm Bob's cause will it?" asked Bradford.

"Actually, I think it may help. As you well know, I dare say, all of Nashville knows Robert Eastin Chapman is my natural son. It's time I publicly acknowledged that fact and have him legitimized before the law and made my heir. It, too, must be done by the General Assembly."

"Robert, this may be your finest hour!"

Mister Bradford stopped in to see Bob and to deliver assurance: "Well, Bob, it won't be long now and you will be a freeman."

"Yes, suh, that's what they tells me. I been waitin' a long time. I been thinkin' 'bout it since Miss Rachel first said I should be free. That was back in '80, over twenty years ago. Miss Olive told me the law had to change. It just been five years since we got our own state. Freedom surely be something worth waiting for."

"You will have to pick a name, you know. Mister Searcy tells me that the first black man in your circumstance was named Jack and his owner named Stone, but the name given him was John Saunders. I would be honored if you used my surname."

"Oh, no thank you, suh. My name is Bob Renfro. Miss Olive told me I always be a Renfro."

"As you wish. You will be a Renfro; however, you will be Robert Renfro."

"I don't know no Renfros name Robert," Bob vowed.

"No, no, no. For legal purposes, you are Robert. You see Bob is just the shortened form of Robert."

"In all my born days I ain't never been named Robert. I swear."

"Let me try a different approach. You have heard men call me Ben? That is a shortened familiar term for Benjamin. Men named William are often called Billy. Joseph is called Joe. I know you've heard men address Andrew Jackson as Andy. If you had been born a free man, your given name would have been Robert and some would call you Bob. You understand?"

"Mister Bradford, if'n you say it be so, it be so. I be Robert in Knoxville and Ole Black Bob in Nashville."

Benjamin J. Bradford had given a lot of thought to the issue of slavery even considering an editorial opinion in his newspaper. The New England states, with the exception of New Jersey, had abolished slavery either in their constitutions or by law. The Northwest Territories did not have slavery, and the twenty-year moratorium imposed by the United States Constitution before Congress took control would be up in seven years. It was not difficult to see that when 1808 arrived, the vote would be to stop the importation of slaves from Africa. But, "what to do with those already here?" That was the question. Slavery was already showing itself to be unprofitable on the small farms in the eastern part of Tennessee; however, the tobacco and cotton crops of the western part required labor. Benjamin Bradford had recently come into possession of a poem that he thought was appropriate to the current situation and would sway more sentiment in Bob's favor.

TENNESSEE GAZETTE
October 07, 1801

TEMPLE OF THE MUSES

The following lines are extracted From European Magazine, and are there said to be attributed to the late moral Poet, William Cowper, esq.

Published at the request of a number of Subscribers

THE NEGROES' COMPLAINT

Forc'd from home & all its pleasures,
   Afric's coast I left forlorn,
To increase a stranger's treasures,
   O'er the raging billows borne

Men from England bot' & sold me'
   Paid my price in paltry gold—
But tho' their's they have enrolled me,
   Minds are never to be sold.

Still in thot' as free as ever,
   What are Englands rights I ask'
Me from my delights to sever,
   Me to torture, me to task?

Fleecy locks and black complexion
   Cannot forfeit nature's claim—
Skins may differ, but affection
   Dwell in white and black the same.

Why did all creating nature,
   Make the plant for which we toil?
Sighs must wait, tears must water,
   Sweat of ours must dress the soil.

Think ye master, iron hearted,
   Lolling at your jovial boards,
Think how many backs have smarted
   For the sweets your cane affords.

Is there, as you sometimes tell us,
   Is there one who reigns on high?
Has he bid you buy and sell us,
   Speaking from his throne, the sky?

Ask him if your knotted scourges,
   Fetters, blood extorting screws,
Are the means which duty urges
   Agents of his will to use?

Hark! He answers! Wild tornadoes,
   Strewing yonder sea with recks,
Wasting towns, plantations, meadows
   Is the voice wherewith he speaks.

He foreseeing what vexations
   Afric's sons would undergo,
Fix'd their tyrant habitations
   Where the whirlwinds answer 'no!'

By our blood on Afric wasted,
   Here our neck received the chain;
By the miseries we have tasted,
   Crossing in your barks the main;

By our sufferings since you bought us
   To the man degrading mart,
Ill-sustained by patience, taught us
   Only by a broken heart.

Deem our nation brutes no longer,
   Till some reason you shall find
Worthier of regard, and stronger'
   Than the colour of our kind.

Slaves of Gold! Whose sordid dealings
   Tarnish all your boasted powers,
Prove that you have human feelings,
   Ere you proudly question our's.

Reaction to publication of the poem was mixed. More slaves were being imported into Nashville to work the big farms. Nevertheless, those operating businesses in the town agreed if it helped Bob's cause it was worth irritating a few farmers.

Richard Cross asked Bob, "You ever been to Knoxville?"

"Well, suh, it depends on how you count it. I ain't been there since it be a town, but I floated by it back in '80. It was about there that Cap'n Blackmore joined up and the redskins started shootin' at us. I guess I just as soon not go back."

"It might help if they meet you and see for themselves what a fine fellow you are," Cross encouraged.

"Judge Jackson took a keg with him. He say, 'That be all them fine gentlemen need to know about Ole Bob'. He say, 'One sip of Bob's finest will convince them.'"

"What are you going to do with yourself once you are emancipated?"

"First off, I going to see Miss Rachel and thank her. All my other old friends be gone 'cept her. Patsy died last year. Miss Olive and Mister Shaw done gone to Kentuck. Next I gonna go downriver to New Orleans 'cause I got a fondness for that place. I need to see some things, learn some things, and maybe buy some things. Mister Searcy gonna rent me this place. Then when I got 'nough, what he calls 'capital,' he gonna sell me a lot, and

I gonna build me a fine tavern. Gen'lemen be able to stay the night or live there perm'nate. That be what I knows and likes the best."

"All of Nashville will be thankful to know we can still go to *Black Bob's Tavern,*" Cross said. After a bit of thought, he added, "I would be careful about traveling. There are very few free colored people. I recommend you travel in the company of a white man."

"I know just the man for that job. That young Phillip Allen is always pestering me 'bout how I cooks things. Says he gonna own a tavern some day. I just hire him to go with me, and he can learn some of that New Orleans cookin'. They do it a little different than we do."

"Good idea. We could use a little more variety," Cross agreed. "More good news, the government has made a deal with the Choctaw and the Chickasaw tribes. That trail to Natchez is going to be improved. Traveling it should be easier and safer."

The Tennessee Constitution required that a bill must be read and passed three times. The petition was received on October 1, 1801. It was referred to the "committee on propositions and grievences" which noted that the petition was "reasonable and ought to be granted." An Act was prepared. Less than six weeks passed before the Act had gone through all of the required steps. With so many influential lobbyists, it encountered no difficulty.

CHAP. XCIII

An ACT to emancipate and set free a negro
Man named Bob.

WHEREAS Robert Searcy, esquire, of Nashville,
      having made known to this general assembly,
That he some time ago purchased said negro man,
Bob, sold under an execution, and that the said negro hath since by his industry, reimbursed the purchase money, in consequence whereof, he prays
that he may be emancipated and forever set free.

BE it enacted by the General Assem-
      bly of the state of Tennessee, That
the said negro man, Bob shall be, and he is hereby
emancipated and forever set free, to all intents and
purposes whatever, and shall in future be known by
the name of Robert Renfro.
                              WILLIAM DICKSON,
              Speaker of the House of Representatives

                                    JAMES WHITE,
                              Speaker of the Senate

PASSED—November 10, 1801

Immediately after the General Assembly legitimized Robert Easton

Searcy and emancipated Robert Renfro, they decided that emancipation

should be empowered in the county courts. A law was enacted requiring a

master to put forth his intentions and motives for manumission and to post a

bond to "reimburse such damages as the county may sustain of such slaves or slaves becoming chargeable." No petition was to be received unless nine members of the county court were present and at least six had to approve of the action. The state's legislative body also passed a law to "prevent the evil practice of dueling."

TEN
DUELS 1803-1806

Bob had gotten his freedom, the thing he treasured most, and Andrew Jackson had gotten what he wanted most, besides Rachel. In February 1802, Jackson had been elected major general of the Tennessee Militia; however, his rank was purchased at a very high cost. Jackson managed to make a bitter personal and political enemy of John Sevier, so much so that Sevier announced his intention to seek the Office of Governor in the next election.

Bob and Phillip Allen had returned from their junket after spending a month sampling the cooking of New Orleans. Phillip Allen was so intent on learning from Bob, he never noticed that he was doing most of the work. Bob continued to emphasize the value of "cook it slow." Young Mister Allen assured Bob that he would not go into competition with him if he continued to instruct him. Shortly after their arrival in Nashville, the two dug a shallow pit in the ground behind Bob's new place. Next they constructed rock walls on all sides of the pit with a opening at one end and had blacksmith Ellis Maddox to build them a grill to fit over the rocks. They used the bottom of a still to fashion a copper hood to cover the grill. The pit was to be used for cooking meats over hot coals, slowly. The cooking of meat over charcoal embers took all night. It required that new coals be added at frequent intervals to keep the temperature at a proper level.

139

Bob knew two methods of removing the bristly hair from hogs. One method was to dip the hog into scalding hot water. The other method was to cover the hog in dry straw and ignite it. The quick burn singed the hog hairs. Bob preferred the scalding method. "If'n you get a good scald on it, ain't nothin' to it," said Bob. The burning process left a smoky taste in the meat that some people thought made it taste even better. The slow cooking over hot coals duplicated that taste. He thought hickory made the best fire, but oak would do. Every now and then, Bob would sprinkle water over some of the burning coals until they were extinguished, collect the coals in a bucket, and take them to his liquor mixing room.

Bob no longer distilled his own liquor. He purchased it from others and mixed it at his place. Being familiar with his suppliers' methods enabled him to produce his own blend. Whiskey was in such high demand that there was seldom time to age it. Bob always blended several kegs to be put aside until it was properly aged to make his sippin' whiskey. It was intended for his personal use, not for the general market. He purchased barrels of a brew called "beer" from Alexander Sheppard, a recent immigrant from Scotland. Sheppard had stayed several years in New York City before migrating to Tennessee. The brew he made was similar to ale and used a heated mash mixture not unlike distilling whiskey, but did not use condensation. As near as Bob could tell, it was the same thing, only different. Beer just had more water in it. But, if that's what the customer wanted, that is what he would be served. Sheppard became Bob's principal supplier of hard apple cider too.

Bob had also developed a sauce to keep meat from drying out when cooking over coals. Apple cider was allowed to turn into vinegar, then red pepper, which had been dried and ground, was added. He doused the meat frequently with the sauce. Generous amounts of salt and pepper were rubbed into to the meat before cooking. He would cook a whole hog, if requested, but his preferred method was to have the hog cut into shoulders, hams, roasts, and loins. He traded away, usually for free labor, the remaining parts of the hog. Heads, feet, ribs, tails, liver, and lights were in demand by some, but Bob wanted only the best cuts of meat on his table. He traded away the lard on halves. He needed lard for frying, now that the supply of bears was all but gone.

"Some folks eats ever'thing but the squeal, then they makes soap out of what's left over," Bob was fond of saying. Bob was partial to hog brains mixed with scrambled eggs. The delicacy was simple to prepare and very tasty. He also kept a supply of "cracklings" on hand by boiling small chunks of the hide with a bit of fat still attached; added to the cornbread mixture, it made "crackling bread."

Once a week Nashville awoke to the aroma of Black Bob cooking pork. He explained to Allen, "It puts a craving on 'em. We sell all we can cook." On other days he prepared his meals using cooking pots known as "Dutch ovens." True to his word, Phillip Allen left Nashville when his self-imposed apprenticeship ended, and went about fifty miles westward to open his own establishment.

In the summer of 1802 Robert Renfro took out advertisements in the *Tennessee Gazette:*

ROBERT RENFROE,
RESPECTFULLY informs his friends
And the public, that he has opened a
House of Entertainment,
In the house adjoining Mr. Joseph
M'Keans store, Nashville, and having
provided himself with the necessary
accommodations for man and horse ,
he hopes from the attention which he
is determined to show those who may
call on him , to merit a share of the
public patronage, and give general
satisfaction.

He included in these advertisements the text of the General Assembly's act emancipating him.

William Ellis dropped in to see Bob. "Bob, I want to do something special for our American Independence Day. We should all celebrate our freedom. Here's what I want you to do—cook me a pork shoulder, and I'll pay extra if you will slow cook me a young goat."

"I be your man," responded Bob. "You just bring me the goat ready for cookin', and I put it on. Have it ready for you in the mornin' on July Fourth. That goat will be some good eatin'. I wouldn't mind a little of it for myself, if'n you got enough. I want to celebrate Independence Day too."

"Done. I'll send for it early on the fourth. You take yourself a goodly portion— as a gift from one free American to another."

The first of many political topics to be discussed at *Black Bob's* was the election in which John Sevier regained the governor's chair. Superior Court Judge Andrew Jackson had gone to Knoxville to hold court. Men had gathered in the common room of the tavern, drawn by the aromatic cooking smells of the day.

"Have your heard the latest?" asked Charles Waters. "Judge Jackson has challenged Governor Sevier to a duel."

"To a duel! Why on God's good green earth would he do that?" asked Preston Hubbard.

"Who knows why Andy does anything when he loses his temper," Waters responded.

David Lamb added what he knew, "I think it all started over that generalship in the militia. Jackson wanted it and so did Sevier. There was a tie vote among the field officers, and Governor Roane cast the deciding vote in favor of Jackson."

"And so, it cost Archibald Roane the election and his job; that's just politics," said Hubbard.

"Not in this case," stated Lamb. "The way I heard it Jackson practically accused Sevier of land fraud and showed Governor Roane papers he thought proved it before the governor cast the deciding vote. Sevier was outraged; that's why he swore to win the next election."

"He had a right to be outraged," said Waters. "We all know John Sevier would not do anything like that."

"More than that," said Hubbard, "John Sevier is a bona fide military hero. He has been victorious in all of his battles. I believe it's over thirty fights. He was a colonel at King's Mountain in the late War for Independence. What has Jackson ever done to make him think he's a general?"

"I believe that the extent of Andy's military experience is Judge Advocate of the Davidson County Militia. He was their lawyer," added David Lamb with a slight smirk.

"That's my point," said Hubbard. "John Sevier deserved the honor."

"How did all this lead to a duel?" asked Paul Hyatt. "I thought dueling was contrary to Tennessee law."

"It is," said Waters, "but that's beside the point. What I was told was that they got in a cussin' fight, and Sevier made an offhand comment about Rachel Jackson."

"Uh oh," said Bob, not waiting to be invited into the conversation. "Judge Jackson can't control his temper when it involve Miss Rachel. The man's brain just boils."

Charles Waters continued to recount the story, as he knew it: "Bob here has hit it square on the head. Andy just went into a rage. He challenged the governor. He sent seconds to the governor's home, and when the governor refused to receive them, he sent written messages. Apparently, the governor decided to ignore the judge, reminding him that Tennessee was a civilized place and had abolished dueling. Now, Andy has published his charges in the newspaper, calling the governor a base coward and a poltroon."

"What be a poltroon?" asked Bob.

"You know old Andy; if he can find a big word to use, he uses it. A poltroon is just a bigger coward than a regular old runaway coward," said Paul Hyatt.

The crowd got a good chuckle out of Hyatt's definition.

144

"Do you think they'll go through with this foolishness?" asked Hubbard.

Charles Waters answered, "Not if they have the common sense they were born with."

The meeting adjourned until further information came from Knoxville.

A week later that information came. There had been a near shooting. The principals had encountered each other again as Jackson was returning from a site he had set for the duel. Swords and pistols were drawn. At some point Jackson had a pistol in each hand as the two men used abusive language on each other. George Washington Sevier, seventeen-year-old son of John, aimed a pistol at Jackson. A Jackson supporter aimed a pistol at the young man, and somehow order was restored.

"Andrew had better let this dog lie," said Charles Waters. "The penalty for dueling in Tennessee is death. If the state doesn't hang him, one of John Sevier's sons or sons-in-law will kill him for sure."

"What happens now?" David Lamb asked.

"Nothing," said Preston Hubbard. "Unless they want to resume this stupidity.

Jackson's ridiculous Gentlemen's Code has been satisfied. He'll think he has proven his point. The governor should continue to ignore Andrew. It'll all go away."

"I sho' hope you right, Mister Hubbard. One of these days Mister Andrew gonna push the wrong man too far and there gonna be the devil to pay," said Bob. "I knowed him a long, long time, but som'time, I swear, the man just can't let well 'nough alone."

II

On September 3, 1803, Robert Searcy left a candle burning in his office. The resulting fire as reported in the newspaper destroyed the "whole of his public and private papers." It also created the need for cash. Twelve days later Robert Searcy and Bob came to an agreement for the purchase of a portion of Lot #25 on Main Street for the sum of one thousand dollars. When Thomas Molloy had laid off the town, most of the lots were to be "20 by 10 poles." Half of such a lot gave Bob 165 feet fronting on Main Street and 165 feet deep. Bob was ready to start the planning and construction of what he believed would be the finest entertainment house in Nashville. He would have the main tavern building, a stable, and a cookhouse with an attached woodshed.

Even as Bob looked after the ongoing construction, business was booming at *Black Bob's Tavern* in November 1803. Bob's reputation as a host had continued to grow. Business rivals respected his having a secret ingredient he added to his whiskey `mixture. It did not keep them from trying to find out, but they respected his right as a businessman. Business was so good that Bob needed extra help. It was usually best to hire slave labor from local owners. Few white men were willing to work for a black man; peer pressure was too much for even the strongest and those most in need of employment. Women of color made excellent bar maids. Through it all, Bob maintained an orderly house. "No foolishness goin' on here, just good food, drinks and discourse," was Bob's constant motto.

Lawyer Charles Dickinson was seated at a table socializing with a few of his friends. Dickinson was about twenty-seven years old, an aristocrat, and well-educated, having studied under Justice John Marshall. He was handsome, well-mannered, and a dapper dresser. For reasons known only to himself, he decided on a show of superiority.

"Innkeeper, I hear you're looking for a boy to help out around here. I might have just the boy for you."

"Yes, suh, I be lookin'. I can't afford no boy outright, but I be willin' to hire one for 'bout a year. Pay good money if'n he smart."

"I'll tell you what I'll do. I'll send you a boy. You keep him for a year. You pay all of his upkeep and at the end of the year you pay me one-hundred dollars."

"Well, suh, that's a might steep for Ole Bob. A hundred dollars is what you pay for a full-growed man. I was thinkin' 'round fifty dollars."

"You must recognize that you have to pay for credit when you pay at the end of the contract. To show you I'm a reasonable man, I'll take eighty dollars at the end of the year, plus another round of drinks for my friends and myself."

"Done."

Dickinson was trapped in a snare of his own making. He could not back down in front of his drinking companions. "I will fill out a promissory note. You just put your mark on it, and it will all be legal. Pour the drinks."

Bob knew that Lawyer Dickinson believed that he had out-bargained him. Truth be told, Bob would have paid the hundred dollars. Once negotiations started, Bob had little choice. Bargaining with a white man was not good policy, but Bob knew from experience that when a man was drinking and trying to impress his friends, he was likely to get a little careless. This knowledge had just saved him twenty dollars.

The next day a slight-built negro boy appeared at the tavern. He looked as though he had been cleaning out a stable and could have used a good scrubbing from head to toe. His clothes were little more than rags, and his feet were bare.

"Massa Charles Dickinson, the lawyer, send me. He say I be yo' boy fer a ye'r."

"Good. What's your name, boy?"

"Elisha."

"How old are you?"

"'Bout fou'teen dey tells me."

"All right, Elisha, you do me a good job, and I treat you right. You get plenty to eat; you sleep in the back room; if'n you need clothes, I'll get you some. From the looks of you, that be the first we do. What did you do for Lawyer Dickinson?"

"I clean out the stables at Cap'n Erwin's place. Sometimes I runs the horses. Mister Dickinson married to the Cap'n's daughter."

Bob gave Elisha instructions on sweeping out the tavern and keeping the woodbox full. At his first opportunity, he arranged for a seamstress to make Elisha two changes of clothes.

"Keep yo'self and yo' clothes clean. When yo' clothes need washin', put them with mine and take them over to Missus Mallory. She do all my washin' and sewin' and don't charge too much."

Elisha proved a willing worker, as well as a quick learner. Bob liked the boy and started to instruct him in the fine art of being a successful tavern operator.

"First thing you gots to know is, all white men have titles, and they want them used."

"What be titles?"

"That's a word that goes 'fore their name. It kind of shows how important they be. You know how you call Cap'n Erwin. Cap'n better than mister. If'n they got a title in the militia, they like it to be used. Old gen'lemen, who got their title in the war, they calls it rank, insist on being called by it. Now som'times you use the title to refer to them and that be a little different than you calls them to their face."

"How that be?"

"Like you can say, 'Good afternoon, Mister Dickinson.' But, if you tell som'one else you say, 'I seen Mister Lawyer Dickinson.' You understand?"

"Not for sure. I see Mister Lawyer Jackson here reg'lar."

"That for sure not right. I admit it be hard to know just what to call him. Judge Jackson probably best for you. Though it be proper to call him Gen'ral Jackson 'cause it be that in the militia. His wife still call him Judge Jackson, so I think that best. He ain't been no judge since last year. Don't you ever call no white man by his familiar name. Don't even think it 'cause next thing you know you be done slipped."

"I thought I hear'd you talk 'bout Miss Rachel and Mister Andrew."

"That be different. I knowed them for twenty-five years or more. But I be careful who I say it to. I knows the rules. I tryin' to 'splain them to you."

"Yes, suh. What I calls you?"

"To start with, you just a boy. You call ever'body older 'mister'. You can't go wrong with mister and massa, if'n you not sure. They will correct you if'n they wants to be called som'thin' else. Make sure you 'member it. Ever'body just calls me Bob."

Yes, suh, Mister Bob."

Bob and Elisha set up Bob's new establishment on Main Street. It was about two-hundred feet to the south of the building he had been renting. It was a wood-frame building with whitewashed plaster walls on the inside. On the first floor was the common room that could accommodate thirty-six guests, more if some didn't mind standing. The tables were made of walnut. There was a small room for private dining and where meetings could be held. Bob's office with sleeping cots for Bob and Elisha and a storage room completed the floor. On the second story were sleeping rooms, six furnished with feather mattresses, a small walnut table, and a chair. Each room had a window. There was also a large room furnished with eight cots for gentlemen who only wanted a place to sleep for a night or two. Cooking would be done away from the main building to guard against fire. Near the cookhouse was a storage building with several rooms. This building contained Bob's favorite room — his mixing-room, where he blended the various whiskeys purchased from the local distillers to get just the taste he wanted. About once each month, when he was sure he was alone and the door barred, he mixed a few kegs of sippin' whiskey and put them aside to age. He never forgot that his agent, Andrew Jackson, had advised him to "never tell anyone…not even your lawyer," how he made it. He gave some thought to having a washhouse, but Mary Frances Mallory assured him that she could continue to take care of the laundry, even if she had to hire additional help. It was a proud day when Bob hung up his sign with an eagle on it. Edward Terrance, a struggling young craftsman, had carved the eagle with wings spread into both sides of a thick oak board.

After a month at the *Sign of the Eagle*, Bob had an idea. He waited until he could talk with Judge Jackson alone.

"Judge Jackson, I needs help with my books and my ordering. I can't remember ever'thin'. I think I got an answer to my problem."

"And what would that be?"

"I wants to get someone to teach Elisha to read and write. You think that be all right?"

"Bob, you sly old fox. I know you can read some. My dear wife told me you had a thirst for learning."

"Yes, suh. But I don't get no practice. I can read labels like Miss Rachel and the Renfro chill'un showed me. It takes me all day to figure what the *Gazette* say. Usually some customer read it out loud, then I can go back and make it out a little."

"I'll tell you what you do. You send that boy to my law office twice a week. I'll have one of my clerks instruct him."

"I thank you, Judge. That's mighty kind. I can pay someone for the lessons."

"Look at it this way. If it's going on in my office, no one will question it. Besides, I will always be in your debt. I wouldn't have my beloved Rachel if it hadn't been for you. I'll pay the clerk myself. He'll be happy to get the extra money. You send me a keg of that sipping whiskey you make."

"Done. I deliver it myself. I got one other thing. I wants to buy this boy. Can you help with that?"

"That'll be tricky. You are a freeman. You have every right to purchase an African, but before you start having Elisha tutored, you should consider what happens if Dickinson will not sell him. And if you are planning on setting him free, you know what a difficult process that is. I don't think there has been a case of a former slave freeing another slave."

"I have thought on all that. I take him and treat him like Miss Olive treated me. When he old enough, well maybe the court say it be all right. Elisha deserves this chance. He is a good boy."

III

Elisha was a quick learner. He quickly grasped the concept of reading and made good progress in making his letters. He had some difficulty with spelling but was improving. Where he excelled was in arithmetic. He had a practical knowledge of how he had been doing arithmetic; he just did not know that was what he was doing. He was able to assist Bob more and more. Bob and Judge Jackson discussed what they thought would be the asking price.

"I don't care what the price. I pay it if'n I got it."

"Don't appear too eager. The price will just go up. Allow me to negotiate on your behalf. That is one of the services lawyers perform for their clients," Jackson cautioned.

In mid-October, Andrew Jackson arrived in the company of John Coffee. He introduced Bob and said, "We're thinking of going into business together. I've been telling Mister Coffee that since you decided to go into the tavern business, I needed a new source for trade goods and a partner."

Bob could not take his eyes from John Coffee. He was the biggest man he had ever seen, even bigger than Prometheus. He was a mountain of a man, about six-feet, eight-inches tall. At last Bob said, "Mister Coffee I gonna need a bigger door if'n you come 'round often."

"We're also going to operate a distillery and a boatyard," said Jackson.

154

"Well, suh, it look like we do lots of business then, kinda like the old days," said Bob.

Jackson and Coffee ate a bowl of stew and made small talk. Coffee left to attend to some business. Jackson was sitting in the small room off the main hall, looking over some papers he had prepared for Bob when Charles Dickinson entered *Black Bob's Tavern*.

"I'm here for the boy Elisha."

"Elisha? I don't understand, Mister Dickinson. I got Elisha for close to another month."

"I want the boy. Mister William Anderson has hired him to ride his racehorse. I'll send you someone else for the remaining time. Pack his clothes."

This last remark particularly riled Bob. The boy had arrived in rags. All the clothes he possessed Bob had purchased.

"Yes, suh, Mister Dickinson. But I put my mark on the note you drew up. You said that made it all legal."

"Are you questioning me? You damn ignorant black savage!"

With this remark, Andrew Jackson burst into the room, his eyes ablaze.

"Dickinson, you scoundrel. How dare you come into this man's place of business and abuse him."

"This is none of your affair, Judge Jackson."

"I am making it my affair. Robert Renfro is a freeman and the proprietor of this tavern. I do some of his legal work. I intend that he be accorded the respect he deserves."

"As I said. This is not your affair." Turning back to Bob, he again ordered that the boy be made ready and stalked out the door.

"What am I to do now, Judge Jackson? He will never sell me the boy now."

"We'll just have to see what develops. Mister Dickinson is a lawyer. He knows a contract when he sees one, particularly when he is the one who drew it up. I'll do everything within my power to help you."

The following day Captain Joseph Erwin presented himself in the tavern.

"I'm here to get the boy Elisha that is the legal property of Mister Charles Dickinson. Get your clothes, boy, and come with me."

Elisha was long conditioned to do what Captain Erwin told him. He quickly put together his bundle and went outside.

"Another boy will be sent to you. This is the end of this. You understand?"

Bob just stood mesmerized. Joseph Erwin commanded respect. Bob knew his only hope was Judge Andrew Jackson.

Judge Jackson advised caution. The ultimate objective was to gain ownership of Elisha. Other developments occurred and the replacement did not come. In January, Bob was served with a legal notice demanding payment of the eighty-dollar note plus an additional two dollars and eighteen cents in interest.

"Damnation on his despicable aristocratic soul. He intends to use this to prove he is a better lawyer than I. Bob, unfortunately you have become a pawn in a lawyer's game," Jackson scorned.

"Yes, suh, but will I get Elisha back?"

"It will take time."

IV

The year 1805 was to be overly eventful. The spring racing season saw the deepening of animosity between Charles Dickinson and Andrew Jackson. Most of Nashville knew of their dislike for each other. It was assumed it had something to do with racing horses. Bob liked the races. He would load up his wagon with hard cider and tasty treats and operate a concession. If he could get lemons, he made ginger beer; two weeks of aging in a wooden cask caused it to be the drink of choice among the ladies. Occasionally, Bob placed a bet with a bookmaker on a horse Andrew Jackson particularly favored. He usually won.

Andrew Jackson considered himself the foremost authority on horseflesh in these or any parts. He bought, sold, bred, raised, trained, and raced thoroughbreds. He wagered large sums, so much so that he often faced financial ruin. This was one of those times. Earlier in the year, Jackson had pledged everything he owned to gain possession of a big stallion named Truxton after the horse had lost to a horse named Greyhound. Jackson was convinced that Truxton was the superior horse. He arranged a rematch as the last event in the spring racing season at Hartsville. Greyhound was the favorite and the odds were increasing. Some gamblers were betting 5-1 against Jackson's horse. The opportunity was too much for Jackson to pass up. After a visit to Bob and a long conversation in the tavern's back room, Andrew Jackson placed a side bet of five thousand dollars on Truxton. Jackson undertook the training of the horse himself. An exceptionally large crowd witnessed Truxton's victory. The collection of the purse by Jackson and his friends was sweet public vindication of his ability to judge horseflesh. The collection of the side bets ended Andrew and Rachel Jackson's financial woes. Once again Andrew Jackson and Bob Renfro were dressed in splendid new clothes.

More controversy arose between Jackson and Dickinson. Oddly, it had something to do with a race that didn't happen. Captain Erwin's horse Ploughboy was to run against General Jackson's horse Truxton in the fall racing season. Captain Erwin had to withdraw because the horse was not fit to run. He was required to pay a forfeit fee to Jackson and his backers. Erwin paid with a promissory note for eight hundred dollars. The value of the note was questioned by Jackson, which only added fuel to a blazing fire. Charges started to appear in the newspapers. Rumors went back and forth. Others got involved and political opportunists saw an opening. Bob could not understand the ways of gentlemen and how they attacked each other with words, particularly in newspapers. It was said Mister Dickinson made some unflattering remarks about Rachel Jackson. When General Jackson called him out, he apologized on grounds that he was drunk at the time. General Jackson accepted the apology and asked Captain Erwin to restrain his son-in-law before he was required to demand satisfaction.

During the same months, Bob was advised to file a counter suit against Charles Dickinson for breach of contract. Judge Jackson had another secret meeting with Bob.

"You'll use Lawyer Whyte for this action."

"What does this mean?"

"It is all part of our plan. You must go to court and file a suit. I can't represent you. I've given up pleading court cases. Nevertheless, the case will go before Judge Overton. Here is what you do. You get with Lawyer Whyte. He will ask the court to hear the oral complaint of one Robert Renfro versus Charles Dickinson."

"I know problems comin' when I called Robert; I rather be Ole Bob."

"You have to be Robert for legal matters. You know that, do you not?"

"Oh, yes, suh, Mister Benjamin Bradford 'splain all that to me. I tell you what I tell him: 'If'n you say it be so, it be so. I be Robert at the courthouse and Bob at the tavern."

"That's right. Now where were we?"

"Filing suit."

Judge John Overton heard Robert Renfro's oral presentation. Bob was given some leeway because he was untrained in the law, but he was a freeman in Tennessee and had the legal right to make his claim. It didn't hurt that Judge Overton was Jackson's friend and law partner. This baffled Bob. Why go to court when your friends are in control? Jackson explained that the judge was sworn to be impartial.

"How can a man not know what he knows?"

"My Rachel told me long ago that you can be the most hardheaded person but with some strange sort of logic, and now I have experienced it myself. It brings back memories of our river voyages."

160

Charles Dickinson refused to dignify the case with a personal appearance. He filed a brief stating his position and asking the court to dismiss the case. He even went so far as to appeal for dismissal to the Superior Court, which sent it back, stating, "An issue cannot be appealed until after it is decided." Judge Overton took the case under advisement before deciding it was too small a claim to be in court. The principles, including Joseph Erwin, should be able to work this out among themselves.

Andrew Jackson was pleased with the results. A black man had made Charles Dickinson have to answer before a court of law. In fact, the highest court in Tennessee, while trying to escape this matter, had rejected Dickinson. Charles Dickinson was not the infallible lawyer he thought he was. Bob knew he had neither won nor lost. He didn't feel he was any closer to obtaining Elisha. He was aware that a meaningful result had been obtained because a court of law in Nashville, Tennessee, had recognized him as the legal equal to any other freeman.

V

The rematch between Ploughboy and Truxton was set for the spring meet. The race was scheduled for April 3 at the Clover Bottom Racetrack on the very land Captain John Donelson first settled in 1780. The race was held on schedule and Truxton won easily. General Jackson was elated. He had the forfeit fee, the purse, and the side bets, which amounted to a considerable fortune. He had, also, rubbed salt in the wounds of his nemesis. Within a short period of time, Charles Dickinson repeated the slander about Rachel Jackson. Jackson's challenge was issued and accepted. This time Judge and General Andrew Jackson agreed to comply with Tennessee anti-dueling law by meeting Dickinson at the often-used dueling grounds in Logan County, Kentucky, on Friday May 30, 1806, seven days hence.

Bob went to see General Jackson at his office and was informed the Judge was at his farm. Bob went to the livery stable where his horse and wagon were kept. This time he rode a saddle horse out of Nashville, past Clover Bottom to the farm the Jacksons. He wanted to avoid Miss Rachel, but he had to see Judge Jackson. He stopped a house servant near the dwelling and asked him to inform his master that Robert Renfro wanted a private meeting with him. Jackson emerged from the house and motioned Bob to a more secluded spot.

"Mister Andrew, I got to ask you not to do this thing with Mister Dickinson. Ole Bob ain't worth gettin' nobody kilt."

"It's more than you, Bob. The cowardly scoundrel has gone behind my back and insulted my wife, even after I gave him fair warning and he assured me that he had no malicious intent. I will let no man live who does me such a disservice. I have every intention of killing the cowardly cur."

"Mister Andrew, you know that this started in my tavern with him showin' off for his friends. Then I got Elisha and it just did not work out to my satisfaction. What he called me don't matter. I been called names 'fore. I be called names again. It just kept gettin' worse. It still ain't worth killin' a man."

"Bob, he just used you and the situation. His intent was to prove himself superior to me all along. Now it will cost him his life."

The futility of the effort was recognized. Bob just shook his head and mounted his horse. "I think you wrong, Mister Andrew. You could go and get yo'self kilt."

"Only one of us will return from Kentucky."

Jackson walked back into his home.

"What did Ole Bob want?" asked Rachel

"Oh, he just wanted to collect on a bet I placed for him."

"Strange, I don't ever remember him not stopping to speak to me."

Bob was heartsick. He could be the cause of the death of Miss Rachel's husband. He had to do something, but what?

The upcoming duel was the only topic of conversation in every place where men gathered to drink. Bob listened intently to every conversation, asked questions, and gathered every scrap of information possible before going to see John Overton. He was ushered in and given a seat in the Judge's office.

"What can I do for you, Robert?" he said in an almost joking manner.

"It be Mister Andrew. You can't let him do this thing; it be just plain wrong!"

"Bob, you don't understand the Gentlemen's Code. Of course, you couldn't. It is not part of your culture. When two gentlemen agree to a duel, neither of them can get out of it. It would be a disgrace that could never be lived down. It can only be settled on the field of honor. My brother Thomas, as a gentleman, will stand with our friend."

"I don't know nothin' about no code. I do know that Mister Dickinson is the best pistol shot in these parts, and Mister Andrew is just a fair shot. If'n it has to be, then we needs to make sure our man win."

"Are you suggesting something? Is it honorable?"

"I don't know and I don't care. You be the judge of that."

"Proceed."

"From what I hear, Mister Dickinson not only the best shot, he the fastest. He will hit what he aims at befo' Mister Andrew even gets his pistol raised. That be the problem."

"And, pray tell, what is your solution?"

"Mister Dickinson is so cock-sure of himself he won't go for the easy shot. He wants a clean shot through the heart. That way he get to brag."

"Robert, it would not be an honorable thing to wear some type of armor."

"Yes, suh. But do the rule say the heart has to be where Mister Dickinson think it be?

"In your estimation, how would that work?"

"I ain't ever seen no duel. What do they wear?"

"Just their regular clothes. Sometimes they remove their coats."

"No, suh. Don't let Mister Andrew take off nothin'. Get him to put on som'thin' bigger, a greatcoat or a cloak. As big as Mister John Coffee wears."

"I'm not following you. Explain a little more, if you would."

"Yes, suh. You ever see a rattlesnake try to bite a turkey. Snake can't do it. He see them feathers and bites where he think the turkey be. Not where the turkey really be."

"I begin to see your logic. If the rascal shoots quickly and aims for where he thinks the heart is, he may be off just enough that he won't kill Judge Jackson. For sure he will be wounded, but he won't be dead. I'll have to think about this. At first glance, I see nothing that violates the rules. You know as well as I that Judge Jackson will not take an unfair advantage."

"Yes, suh, but he don't have to know. You be savin' yo' friend's life."

"Robert, do not discuss this with anyone else, ever! Do I have your promise?"

"Like you had me say in your court, Judge: 'I take a oath on all the holy evangelists of Almighty God.'"

Larry Michael Ellis

VI

Andrew Jackson was wounded. Charles Dickinson was dead. As usual, word filtered into Nashville in several versions. "Jackson murdered the man." "It was a fair fight; Dickinson knew the rules." "Jackson got an extra attempt." "Minutes passed between the time Dickinson fired, and Jackson took deliberate aim and killed an unarmed man." "He shot Jackson. Jackson was within his rights to take his time."

Bob was pleased that his friend was alive. He felt sorry that Cap'n Erwin's daughter was now a widow with a baby on the way. He let his mind drift: "She might just need money, and that would be my chance to get Elisha. But Judge Jackson was to take care of that. No Dickinson would deal with Andrew Jackson. There has to be a way, and Mister Andrew will know it. I'll give him some mindin' time befo' I go to see him."

Two weeks later, Bob found the wounded Andrew Jackson sitting in the sun. He noted that the wound was just to the side of the heart.

"How you feeling, Mister Andrew?"

"I'm improving every day. The doctor wants to leave the ball in me. That's some keepsake of a dark day."

The two old friends just sat and made small talk. After awhile, Rachel joined them with three glasses and a pitcher of cider that had been cooled in the springhouse. They talked and laughed for an hour. Bob would not bring up business with Miss Rachel present.

"Walk with me to the garden, Bob," Rachel said.

"Bob, I have a question for you. When the Overtons brought my husband home, I was thanking them for all they did. Judge Overton said, 'Don't thank me; thank Robert Renfro.' What did he mean by that?"

"Lawdy, Missy, I don't know. You know Ole Bob always talkin' some mess. I just don't know. You know I had a case again' Mister Dickinson in Judge Overton's court. Maybe he mean som'thin' 'bout that."

"Even you! My oldest friend and you won't tell me the truth. Men always stick together. You do know that just infuriates women?"

They rejoined Judge Jackson. Rachel said, "Dearest, have you noticed that Bob is starting to gray? It gives him such a distinguished look. I think it is time for us to start calling him 'Uncle Bob.' Don't you agree?

"High time. We respect no man more. 'Uncle Bob' it shall be."

"I thank you both. You knows that I hold you in the highest regard," a slightly embarrassed Bob mumbled in a choked voice. "I best be getting' back to town."

Bob was well aware that he had just moved up in respectability.

Bob had come on a wagon this time. "Anythin' you want me to haul for you?"

"No, thank you, Uncle Bob," Jackson paused, "and, Uncle, I haven't forgotten that other matter. It will be taken care of. You go talk to Robert Searcy."

"What other matter?" demanded Rachel.

"Just some more business, Missy," said Uncle Bob.

"Men!"

ELEVEN
TREASON – 1807

It was still bitterly cold in late February 1807. At *Black Bob's Tavern* breakfast was over, and the tavern had been cleaned. Elisha was browsing through the newspaper. "Mister Bob," he said, "you remember that Mister Burr that come in here with Gen'ral Jackson a while back?"

"'Course I remember him. He been here two, no, three times. First time there was big celebrations about such a impor'ant gen'leman comin' to Nashville. Stayed out at Gen'ral Jackson's farm. Other times, Gen'ral Jackson sent word to set up the back room, fix up some slow-cooked smoked pork and sweet potatoes, make some fresh corncakes. He liked it all. Said he never ate finer. Why you ask?"

"Paper says he been arrested."

"What for?"

"Treason!"

Bob's recollection was not what he wished. Aaron Burr's visit to Nashville had occurred during the same time period as the controversy with Charles Dickinson. He remembered that Aaron Burr had been Vice President of the United States when Mister Thomas Jefferson was the President. He remembered, too, the talk about Mister Burr having killed a Mister Alexander Hamilton in a duel. Bob thought, "Maybe it was him that put the dueling notion in Andrew Jackson's head. No, Andrew Jackson didn't need no help with that idea." Bob didn't have to wait long until the men who had gathered at his place for ten years to debate issues were in attendance.

"The most bizarre thing I ever heard of," offered Charles Waters. "The man was Vice President of these United States, and he now stands accused of treason."

"It's more politics," said Preston Hubbard. "You recall even John Sevier got accused of treason. When the politicians don't agree with you, they accuse you of something despicable."

"From what I gather, he did something despicable," Paul Hyatt proclaimed. "He plotted to attack Spain, take over New Orleans, and set up his own empire on the Mississippi."

The mention of New Orleans heightened Bob's interest. "Why would the gen'leman do somethin' like that?" Bob asked.

"Land and more land," answered David Lamb. "All of these so-called gentlemen are obsessed with the acquisition of land. They see themselves as kings."

"That's a little harsh, David," said Waters. "Do you really think they see themselves as kings?"

Hubbard added, "He may be off on the king part, but not the land. Land is the key to untold wealth. We are all here today because men seeking land came to the Cumberland."

David Lamb turned to Bob and asked, "Didn't Andrew Jackson have some private meetings with Mister Burr and others here?"

"If'n he did, they still be private," retorted Bob.

"You won't get anything about Jackson out of Bob," said Charles Waters. "Bob thinks Old Andy makes the sun come up."

"No, suh," Bob interjected, "that not 'xactly true; maybe the moon, but not the sun."

Once more Bob had managed to deflect the conversation away from himself using his good nature and humor.

"Well, what was Burr doing here if he wasn't trying to get Jackson to help him with his scheme?" Paul Hyatt surmised. "We sometimes forget just how important and influential Jackson is. He's been a lawyer, a judge, and a member of both houses of the Congress. He is personally acquainted with our national leaders, and don't forget he commands the militia."

"I wouldn't go too far with this conspiracy theory, Paul, unless, of course, you're willing to go to the dueling grounds," said Hubbard, intending the remark to be dry humor.

"I'm not sure Paul would meet Andy's gentleman criteria," said Waters. "Remember Jackson took a cane to young Thomas Swann when he got involved with the Dickinson challenge. Said Swann wasn't a gentleman. Took after John Sevier with a cane too. Now, that's not to say Paul wouldn't meet Andy's criteria for a caning."

"Not funny," said Hyatt. "Could we get back to the subject at hand? What happens with Burr now?"

"Now there is a question I can answer," said Hubbard. "He'll be taken to Richmond for trial."

171

Hubbard took a sip of his drink and after a brief pause continued, "Let's not overlook the fact that General Jackson did put the militia on alert. He put out all that information about the need to be prepared against the Spanish. Same argument he put out three years before."

"That is true," agreed Waters. "At the time I thought it was a clever ploy to divert talk away from the Dickinson affair. Now, I'm not so sure. Surely, he wouldn't call out the Tennessee Militia to help Aaron Burr attack a country at peace with the United States."

David Lamb said, "My understanding is that Burr had assembled an army. There has been quite a bit about this over the last year or so. The Ohio Militia seized some of his boats. Didn't he get several boats from Jackson and John Coffee? The Navy has orders to intercept Burr's boats at New Orleans. General James Wilkinson, the Governor of the Louisiana Territory, is a friend of Burr's. I heard he was in it with Burr but has since turned on him. I'm surprised that no one else is being indicted. It seems to me it is difficult to have a conspiracy with only one person."

The debate for the evening came to a close. The trial would provide months of conversation and debate. Bob's hope was that Andrew Jackson was not involved, but he knew that there was very little Jackson wouldn't do for prestige and wealth. Land would give him both. If he was offered a lot of land...well, Bob just didn't know.

Bob had put himself on alert when the militia was alerted because Robert Renfro was a freeman in Davidson County, Tennessee. That fact alone made him eligible for military service. He wasn't sure what his age was, but he was reasonably certain he wasn't fifty years old. If he were needed, he would go. Back in 1803, when General Jackson put the militia on alert, Bob thought he might have to shut down his business and go downriver with Andrew Jackson one more time. It didn't concern him that his business would have to be sold or abandoned; it was the duty of a freeman to serve in the militia. He recalled that the alert in '03 had something to do with land, also. President Thomas Jefferson had purchased land west of the Mississippi River from the French. It made New Orleans American. The Spanish and English objected. John Sevier ordered that the militia be prepared to march. Nothing ever came of it; however, Jefferson sent Merriweather Lewis and William Clark to explore the new territory that almost doubled the size of the United States' lands. Bob speculated on the obsession of some with land. "I got me this little piece of land for as long as I live. This one little piece is 'nough for me. Moses in the Bible and Moses Renfro, they took out lookin' for land and Moses died and Mister Renfro got a lot of people kilt before they reached the Promised Land. Gen'ral Jackson wants land. His foolishness cost him that Hunter Hill place. Now Miss Rachel workin' her fingers to the bone out at that Hermitage place just 'cause they want to own a big piece of land. It's all 'bout ownin' land."

II

The Cumberland College Crowd, as Bob now referred to his regulars, were beginning to gather for their usual discussions on current events. Cumberland College had succeeded Davidson Academy as Nashville's institution of higher learning during the past year.

"This thing is going nowhere," declared Preston Hubbard. "I've read the indictment. It only deals with the events at Blannerhassett's Island up on the Ohio. It doesn't say anything about meetings in Washington, Nashville, Natchez, or New Orleans. That is where the witnesses would be."

"I wouldn't say it's going 'nowhere,'" injected David Lamb. "After all, President Jefferson has a personal interest in the case. It is being tried in the Virginia District, and Justice John Marshall ruled there was enough information for an indictment."

"One thing appears certain," said Charles Waters, "Andrew Jackson is in the clear for now. He may have been a part of Burr's masterplan, but he had nothing to do with anything north of here."

"Andrew Jackson always has an escape," said Paul Hyatt. "Our General Jackson has others hanged; he does not get himself hanged. I'm not sure whether he is the craftiest man alive or just the luckiest."

Bob thought about that remark. He didn't know either. He had overheard General Jackson tell John Coffee that what Colonel Burr had in mind was not treasonous, but if the government could prove treason, they should hang Burr. The person Jackson most wanted hanged was General

Wilkinson. In his opinion, Wilkinson was secretly in the employ of the Spanish; he agreed with Burr and then turned on him to save his own hide.

Waters added, "Once more you gentlemen are getting too far ahead of the events. Jackson has a summons to appear. He could still be in for some trouble."

Hubbard had studied the case thoroughly, and he intended to be heard: "To get back to the Burr case, last year they tried to get him in Kentucky; the grand jury exonerated him. They arrested him in the Mississippi Territory; again, a grand jury refused to indict. Now we move to Virginia. It will not be any different. I keep telling you gentlemen, it is just politics as usual. To be convicted of treason, the Constitution of the United States of America requires two witnesses to the same overt act. He may be guilty of political sins, but what they have will not stand up before honest jurors."

In early September the news came that a jury found Aaron Burr was "not proved to be guilty under this indictment by any evidence submitted to us."

"Well, suh, we sure had us some excitement 'round here," said Bob. "Wonder what them gen'lemen gonna find to talk 'bout now? It suit me just fine if things just slow down for 'bout five years. Ever since we left Virginny, it just been one thing after another. I might just go to New Orleans and see if'n it changed as much as here. I don't need nothin' though. Nowadays, you can get most ever'thing right here in Nashville and sell whatever you got too. Ain't no need to go nowhere. 'Course there be other reasons to see New Orleans."

"Mister Bob, you can't go nowhere," Elisha interrupted. "Gen'ral Jackson didn't get in that trial, but it say in the paper he made a speech in Richmond. Called the Pres'dent ever'thing but a child of God. Now the British done attack a 'Merican ship. Kilt a bunch of sailors. You knows how the Gen'ral hates them English."

"I sho' do. He hold them responsible for lot of bad things happened to him when he was 'bout your age. The man do carry a grudge. Yes, suh, the gen'lemen from the college gonna have plenty to talk 'bout."

After a few minutes of deep thought Bob said, "My new notice in the paper?"

"Yes, suh, right here," Elisha said, shoving the paper toward Bob.

NOTICE

The subscriber begs leave to inform
the public and friends in general
that he yet continues to keep up his
BOARDING—HOUSE
as usual on Main Street, in Nashville at the sign
of the EAGLE : where he has established the
following rates where his former customers
and strangers will be thankfully received, and
due attendance paid them.

Genteel boarders per year	130 dolls.
Boarding & lodging per week	3 do.
Horses per week	2 do.
Horses for 24 hours	50 cs.

ROBT. RENFRO.

TWELVE
ANOTHER RESCUE – 1812

On June 18, 1812, the United States House of Representatives voted to declare war on the United Kingdom of Great Britain and Ireland and the dependents thereof. The vote was along sectional lines. The War Hawks of Tennessee, Kentucky, Ohio, Georgia, and South Carolina cast forty votes for the war and zero against. Connecticut, Rhode Island, and Delaware did not cast a single vote supporting the war. The majority of representatives from New York, New Jersey, and Massachusetts were opposed. New Hampshire, Vermont, Pennsylvania, Maryland, Virginia, and North Carolina had majorities in favor. The final vote was seventy-nine for the war, forty-nine against the war.

For almost a year the war news had not been good. Bob Renfro was busying himself around his place of business when he heard the door open. He looked up and recognized his guest, "Well, good mornin' to you, Gen'ral Jackson. I ain't seen you in a month of Sundays."

"Good morning, Uncle Bob. How are you this fine morning?" asked Andrew Jackson.

"Couldn't be better. How is Miss Rachel?"

"She's well. Sends her regards."

"That always good to hear. What bring you to town?"

Jackson looked around to confirm that no one else was in the room. "I'm meeting with some militia officers. My aide-de-camp, Colonel Thomas Benton, should be here soon. You know him, don't you?"

"Oh yes, suh. He be a lawyer from down in Williamson County. Fine man."

"One of the best," Jackson agreed.

They exchanged small talk for a while until Jackson said, "You know, of course, I've been to Natchez again."

"Yes, suh. Don't much go on that ain't talked 'bout here. You took a whole bunch of my best customers with you. I thought I might just close up and go too. That was 'til it snowed, and I saw the river done froze. Yes, suh, it must have been a cold trip. Awful hard on them boys. Now, I hears you mad with the Pres'dent again."

"Mad is an understatement. Infuriated would be more accurate. We declare war on England—and rightfully so; they would have us be subject to them again—the Governor calls out the militia, and now it appears those fools in Washington have decided to ignore the war. President Madison is not being well-served by his War Department and General Wilkinson. I've warned them for years about what a traitorous dunderhead James Wilkinson is. We should have been sent to recapture Detroit. Instead, they delay and then send us to Natchez. When we get there, we do nothing but drill. Then I'm ordered to disband my army five hundred miles from home without pay or rations. The whole time, England's ally Spain is sitting on our southern border. We should have taken Florida. The insanity of it all!"

Bob had heard the story many times in the discussions held in the tavern. General Jackson had mustered the militia on December 10, 1812, after Governor Blount had sent out the call for eighteen hundred volunteers. Twenty-five hundred men came to the rendezvous on the banks of the Cumberland at the northern terminus of the Natchez Trace. The War Department accepted two thousand and seventy of the Tennessee volunteers. Major General Andrew Jackson had his two regiments of infantry board boats for the often-traveled downstream journey. Brigadier General John Coffee led the regiment of mounted cavalry down the Natchez Trace bound for New Orleans.

General Andrew Jackson, in the name of serving his country, had accepted a subordinate position under General James Wilkinson. Wilkinson had no intention of allowing Jackson to enter New Orleans at the head of an army. He sent a message to Jackson requesting him to stop at Natchez. General Jackson honored the request from his commanding officer and encamped his troops. He cooled his heels in Natchez until February 6 when he received a message from the War Department dismissing him and his troops from "public service" and telling him to "accept for yourself and the Corps the thanks of the President of the United States."

General Andrew Jackson respectfully refused the order to disband his troops so far from home. He vowed he would return his army to Tennessee at his own expense, and, if necessary, they would kill and eat their horses on the way. He demanded and received twenty days' rations from the quartermaster at New Orleans. Eleven wagons were hired at a personal cost of one thousand dollars to carry those that had become so ill they could not march. Jackson, himself walked leading his horse, now being ridden by sick soldiers. Andrew Jackson had left Tennessee a respected militia leader; he returned a beloved military hero, even though they had not seen battle.

"Here be Co'nal Benton now," Bob announced.

Thomas Hart Benton was not yet thirty-three years old. He had been born in North Carolina but spent his formative years in Williamson County, Tennessee. Educated at the University of North Carolina, he was the most successful lawyer in the county south of Nashville. He and his younger brother Jesse were long time admirers of Andrew Jackson as a judge and as their militia leader.

"Good morning, General Jackson. I trust I haven't kept you waiting?" he said.

"On the contrary, Uncle Bob and I were reliving old times. Did you know Bob here came with Colonel John Donelson and my Rachel in '80?"

"Yes, sir. I've had the privilege of hearing his oratory when he recounts his adventures. He's quite a raconteur."

"Thank you, suh. It all be true. You should hear some of the things me and the Gen'ral done."

"We'll dispense with that, if you don't mind," General Jackson said. Then he added, "Let us go to the back room where we won't be disturbed. Uncle Bob will bring us some food, and later we'll have a drink. Hot coffee and bread with some apple butter for now."

As they waited for their coffee to be poured, Jackson's thoughts wandered back to his first voyage with Bob. A wry smile crossed his face. "By the way, Colonel," he said. "Don't let Ole Bob fool you. When it suits his purpose, he can be as eloquent with the English language as any lawyer you ever met and can debate with the best of them."

"I've suspected as much," said Benton. "He seems to be a remarkable man."

Before Jackson could respond Bob delivered the refreshments and then excused himself. Once left alone General Jackson outlined a plan that he wished Colonel Benton to deliver to Washington. He had definite ideas on the prosecution, or, to be more accurate, the lack of prosecution of the war. He also wanted his soldiers paid and his expense money reimbursed. In addition, Andrew Jackson wanted a commission in the regular army of the United States of America.

"That's a tall order, General Jackson. I'll put your plan before all who will listen. It is only right that our troops be paid and that you should be reimbursed your expense money. Getting commissions in the regular army is another thing. What rank do you propose?" asked Benton.

"We won't settle for less than we are now. Major general for me and lieutenant-colonel for yourself."

"General Jackson, if I'm not mistaken, there is no higher rank in the regular army than major-general."

"It is what we deserve. I'll not serve under another imbecile like Wilkinson. Remind them that the only successful military operation to date has been the deployment and return of our militia. It is immaterial that there was no battle. The planning—the execution of the plan—and all in the dead of winter, are our credentials."

"Yes, sir, I shall leave within the week."

181

II

Most of Nashville's laboring class were engaged in harvesting and storing the crops in early September 1813. They valued rest more than meeting with their cronies. Members of the gentry were gathered at the Nashville Inn and the City Hotel. Robert Renfro had the newspaper, *The Democratic Clarion & Tennessee Gazette* spread out before him. Elisha had read the news to him earlier, so Bob was practicing his own reading by looking at the advertisements, most of which he had seen many times before. He sounded out each as he perused the pages: "Talbot's Hotel," "The Nashville Inn," "Bell Tavern," "David Irwin & Co. Iron Mongers," "Bradford's Tennessee Almanac for the year 1813," "Corn Shelling Machine," "Bricklayers," "Carpenters," "New Museum of Wax Work … with likeness of Gen. George Washington, Thomas Jefferson, Bonaparte, Gen. Hamilton & Col. Burr," "Slaves," and "Runaway Slaves." The Talbot ad stated it was at the "Sign of the Eagle." Bob didn't know why Thomas Talbot had decided to use an eagle too. The design was different, but still it was confusing. So, he abandoned the "Eagle" and took the "Cross Keys" as his sign. Bob was particularly fascinated with one advertisement. He didn't have to read it, for he had committed it to memory:

Entertainment

The subscriber being still encouraged of the patronage of a generous public, to persue that line of business which he has been engaged in for 15 or 20 years, he respectfully informs the citizens that he still occupies that convenient and noted stand on main street, Nashville, at the sign of the cross-keys, his stable room is spacious and commodious, but to render it more so, additional buildings are contemplated which shall be bountifully supplied with every kind of provender that can be furnished in the vicinity of Nashville, an attentive ostler will continually be kept, and every attention shall be paid to the well feeding, currying and watering of horses which is regularly attended three times a day, good cooks are provided and his table shall be furnished with every luxury and dainty which Nashville market can afford, a sober, steady & accommodating Bar-keeper is procured & every other perquisite necessary to render guest comfortable, and what will contribute to their quite, is his old and uniform custom of not entertaining any dissipated or disorderly guest, which will not be departed from, & for bill of cost, or terms of boarding cheaper I believe than any other place, ($5 per week for man and horse,) he tenders his grateful thanks to the public for their former custom, and hopes for continuation of their favours which will be thankfully acknowledged by

Robert Renfroe

.

He put the paper aside when a few of his usual patrons began to assemble for eating, drinking, and swapping stories.

"You know, Colonel Benton is back, and Old Tom is mad as a hornet with the General," said Charles Waters.

"I think Billy Carroll shooting Jesse Benton in the arse is the funniest thing I've heard lately. And, all of it with Andy Jackson holding Billy's coat," commented Paul Hyatt.

"Even so, Tom ain't taking kindly to the General standing with Carroll in that asinine duel," added newcomer James Powers. "You know all of them fellows, Bob. What do you hear happened?"

Bob had been waiting for his cue. Over the years he had developed a habit of not entering a conversation until he was invited, and he watched his story telling carefully so as not to take sides. He relished in telling tales. He couldn't count the times he told about how he came to Nashville, the settlement at Renfro Station, and the Battle Creek Massacre, as the attack site had become known. When Bob, the storyteller, spoke, his speech pattern changed to one that white folks expected and enjoyed. In Bob's opinion, "talkin' black" was good for business.

"Y'all knows de Gen'ral takes pride in bein' a gen'leman. Well, in this here mess, he just got trapped. Cap'n Carroll and young Masser Benton got to fussin' over some little som'thin' or other. From what I hears, at first it was not even dem two mad with each other. Next thing you knows, Masser Benton done challenged Cap'n Carroll to a duel."

One of the listeners interrupted, "That Jesse Benton always was a hot-headed nincompoop." The others nodded in agreement before one of them prompted, "What happened then?"

Bob poured each man another cup and picked up his money before continuing, "Well, suh, Cap'n Carroll ask de Gen'ral to do da talkin' and git dis here silliness stopped. 'Fo' he could turn 'round good, dey's on de way to Kentuck and Cap'n Carroll ain't got nobody to stand with 'em. De Gen'ral says som'times a gen'leman has to do things even if he don't likes it, so he stands with de Cap'n. Youse knows de rest. Masser Benton don't hit nothin' and kinda leans over. Boom! He gets a shot in his sit-down place. He be mo' shamed than hurt."

"Maybe so. But that won't help much with Tom Benton. He only went to Washington City as a favor to General Jackson, trying to get his expense money back," said Powers.

Before the discussion could go any further, Malcolm Terrell, the local ner-do-well, burst through the door. "The Bentons done kilt Gen'ral Jackson!"

III

Bob wasted no time in getting to the Nashville Inn. The crowds parted for him. They knew that when it came to looking out for General Andrew Jackson, no one was more trusted than Bob Renfro. Bob saw that several doctors and the massive figure of General John Coffee were tending a bleeding General Jackson. Blood-soaked mattresses and rags lay strewn throughout the room.

"I believe we've got the bleeding stopped. An artery has been severed, the bone shattered; we may have to take the arm off. We'll just have to wait and see," proclaimed one of the doctors.

Bob knelt beside the bed. Sensing his presence, Jackson stirred and opened his eyes. Bob moved closer. He knew his General had words for his ears only.

Jackson began to whisper, "Uncle Bob, you tell Rachel they haven't killed me yet. I'll recover from this too. And you tell these kind doctors I intend to keep my arm."

Bob nodded, gave the doctors their message, and then went outside to find his boy Elisha.

"Elisha, you go out to the farm as fast as you can; take a horse. Tell Miss Rachel that Gen'ral Jackson ain't been kilt. He be bad-off, but he alive, and Ole Bob will see to it he stay that way." With that done, Bob went back inside and checked on his friend's condition again before moving about trying to piece the night's events together. He heard it all from "murder" to "clear self-defense."

Rachel Jackson arrived at the Nashville Inn by carriage early the next morning. After seeing her husband and talking with the doctors, she sent for Robert Renfro. When they were alone she asked, "What happened, Uncle Bob?"

Bob did not take on airs with Rachel Jackson; they had known and respected each other far too long. Nor did he talk in a way other than what came to him naturally.

"I'm not sure, missy. I picked up a lot of talk."

Rachel held up her hand. "I know all about the unpleasantness between William Carroll and Jesse Benton. I even know you advised Andrew to stay out of it 'cause no good could come from it. I know, too, that Thomas Hart Benton was upset. I dare say he had a right to be. You would think that responsible men, militia officers all, would have enough sense to know that when the State of Tennessee outlawed the practice of dueling, it did so for good reason. I just want to know how it came to a shooting between men that had been such good friends."

"Yes'm. The way I puts it together, Gen'ral Jackson and Gen'ral Coffee went into the City Hotel, 'cause that where the Benton brothers was. It all happened so fast you can get any story you wants to believe. All of them shoots their pistols off. That nephew of yours, Stockley Hays, he tried to knife Masser Jesse. I think it was Masser Jesse who shot Gen'ral Jackson. Lawdy, if Masser James Sitler hadn't covered the Gen'ral with his own body, Masser Tom would have kilt him sho' 'nough. Then Gen'ral Coffee take charge, and they take the Gen'ral to the Inn and gets all the doctors they can. They was going to cut his arm off 'til he said, no!"

"What you didn't say was that they were all liquored up and not one of them used any judgment at all. Now Tom Benton will have to leave Nashville or be lynched by a drunken mob. We all lose a friend, and Tennessee loses one of her most promising young men. I've heard Andrew say that himself."

IV

General Jackson, now carrying two pistol balls in his body, was soon pronounced fit enough to be moved to his home, the Hermitage. Bob offered the usual, "If'n you needs me, you knows where I be." He didn't expect to be needed so soon. Two weeks later word reached Nashville of a massacre at Fort Mims, Mississippi Territory. Chief Red Eagle led Creek warriors on the raid that killed two hundred and fifty settlers. Chief Red Eagle was a seven-eighth white man named William Weatherford who chose to follow his one-eighth Creek heritage. Jackson, on hearing the news, exclaimed, "These people must be saved." The Governor of Tennessee, Willie Blount, sent for General Jackson; Rachel sent for Bob Renfro.

"Uncle Bob, I must ask your help again. I want you to accompany General Jackson. He is not fit to travel, but nothing will keep him from going. He's already sent the word that he will command in person."

"Yes, ma'm, that's why they say he be as tough as hickory after that business at Natchez earlier. Yes'um, he be as tough as old hickory and less likely to bend." Bob began to plead his case, "Miss Rachel, I don't wants to go. You knows I hates redskins as much as any freeman in Tennessee, but I be gettin' on in years. I'm just not up to it."

Rachel was well-prepared for Bob's reluctance. "Where else can I turn? My husband trusts you. He knows you're the best camp cook in Tennessee. You're a freeman so you are a member of the militia. By God, it's your duty!" Rachel declared.

189

Bob knew that for him to try to refuse Rachel Jackson anything she wanted was beyond his mortal power. When she got riled enough to invoke the Almighty, all of Bob's resistance ceased. He didn't bother to tell Miss Rachel that he had long since passed the age of required militia service. It flattered him that she still thought of him as that strapping youth that had pulled her from the river.

Bob told Elisha, "I'm going off with the militia. You take care of this place just like I was here. I don't know when or if'n I be back. If anything happens to me, you know where I keeps my money and papers. Mister Searcy drew up a paper that says you be a freeman. But you ain't twenty-one yet. You take that paper and some of the money and leave Nashville."

"But Mister Bob," protested Elisha, "what about your business?"

"Won't be no business. When I bought the lot from Mister Searcy, it say when I'm dead the property goes to his son."

"That don't seem fair," said Elisha.

"When I built my place, it didn't make no difference. I didn't have nobody, so I didn't care what it said. It still don't make no difference. There is plenty of money. You pay anybody that say, 'Bob owes me money;' take what be left and go."

"Go where? I ain't never been nowhere but here," Elisha whimpered, feeling lost and abandoned.

"I've hear'd a lot 'bout a city back East called Boston. Mister Bradford use to tell me 'bout it. You might go there. If'n it be me, I go to New Orleans. Just get on the boats leavin' Nashville regular and float down. When you get there, you look up Mister Ira Lacy. He a freeman with a place like mine. He got a pretty sister too. I stayed at his house when I was down there. He'll help you. Tell him I sent you."

There was an early light frost on the ground when the twenty-five hundred men of the Second Division of the Tennessee Militia mustered late in September. Bob had turned the tavern over to Elisha. Now he stood with the other free negro males. Some carried rifles. Bob had one of his pots, wooden spoons, a good knife, and a few spices. Most knew they would be assigned camp duties, mostly as cooks or as orderlies to officers who didn't bring a slave with them. Still, they secretly hoped for the chance to show themselves as soldiers when the fighting came. They listened to the talk that this would be the last great battle. Once General Andrew Jackson was unleashed, he would vent all his frustration from the Natchez disappointment on these murdering Indians, not stopping until total victory was achieved and the renegade Weatherford hanged.

The young officers looked at Bob and talked among themselves as to what Old Black Bob was doing there. By the time the senior officers arrived, Rachel's friends had made known her wishes to them. Bob left Nashville riding on a supply wagon. He was in an infantry regiment of the Second Tennessee Division. Being known as the General's man did have some advantages. General Jackson joined his division a few days later as it neared the state boundary. His eyes immediately came to rest on Bob Renfro sitting on the wagon. "Come to my headquarters," he ordered. Within the hour Bob was face-to-face with his friend and commander. "Just what in thunderation are you doing here; you are no youngster. Why, you've more gray hair than I do. You should have been excused."

Well, suh, I be a free male in Davidson County, so I's goin' to help you kill Indians. It be high-time to put a stop to their murderin' ways. I seen them do the devil's work for thirty-five years. I wants to be in the final battle."

"Well spoken, Private Robert Renfro. Make that Corporal Renfro," Jackson said, as he softened his tone. "I know my dear wife asked you to come along and look after me. To be honest, I welcome you. I know I'll be well cared for. You'll be assigned to my mess. Dismissed!"

Bob walked away thinking, "Yes, suh, that be where I belong, 'cause if there ever was a mess, Gen'ral Andrew Jackson be it."

Sometimes the ailing general joined Bob on the wagon, but just to rest a little. Andrew Jackson would do nothing to show weakness before his men. When he rode the wagon, he pretended to study maps and make notes. Late at night, after the camp was asleep, Bob would make sure General Jackson was resting well before he retired, only to be the first one up and have breakfast ready the instant *his General* wanted it. The fall mornings were chilly and a hot meal was important to start the day for a now recovered, but still weak General Jackson. Under Bob's care he was strong again by November when the fighting started.

Bob did not understand all the strategy, especially how Cherokees and a few Creeks became Jackson's allies. He did understand young David Crockett's report, "We shot 'em down like dogs," when troops under General Coffee attacked the Red Stick village of Tallushatchee. Not a warrior escaped. Eighty-four women and children became captives. Among them, General Jackson spotted a toddler wandering aimlessly, ignored by the women. "You there, take care of that child," he shouted at one of the squaws. She turned with defiance to the mounted victor, "Take care of him yourself; you killed his parents! He will be better off dead."

V

"Look at this little tyke," a beaming Andrew Jackson said to no one in particular. "He's not afraid of anything." The lad was indeed handsome; dressed in deerskins and a narrow headband, he looked like a miniature warrior. Understanding that he was the center of attention, he was standing as tall as possible, his black eyes ablaze, and his raven-black hair flowing about his shoulders. He won the General over when he accepted the sugar water Jackson had mixed himself. Then he accepted the stew Bob offered.

"How old do you think he is? I guess about two, maybe three; my son will be five next month. And now this lad is without a mother or a father to guide him. I know what that's like, and I'm going to do something about it," the General pledged.

"Yes, suh, I knows, too," Bob mumbled. His thoughts wandered to his past. As a youth, he could never remember having a blood-relative. Somewhere he remembered someone telling him he was descended from the kings of Africa, but he never knew a black man nor an Irish man who didn't make the same claim. In his earliest memory, he was already in a white family, although not quite fitting in. Bob never dwelled much on this subject; to him it was simply the way things were. It was neither good nor bad; it just was. It crossed his mind that he might have been a companion for someone, even before William Renfro. White folks put a lot of store in their children having someone near their own age to play with. But what happened to that boy? Maybe he died. Bob just could not remember.

Jackson dismissed his staff officers. "Uncle Bob," he lapsed into the familiar term, "I want you to take the boy to my wife at Nashville. Tell her…" he trailed off. "Never mind, I'll put it in a letter. You can leave with the dispatch officer tomorrow morning."

"Well, boy, I guess I gonna be yo' Uncle Bob too. It won't do you no good to think otherwise. When Gen'ral Jackson say you goin' to Miss Rachel, you be on yo' way. She ain't got no nat'ral chill'n. She got one boy her cousin done give her. The one they call Andrew Jackson, Junior. She be glad to have you too. She do luvs chill'n. We better see if'n we can find out yo' name."

There was a colored woman among the Creek prisoners who had been captured in Georgia two years before. She had never tried to escape because it made little difference to her if she was a slave of the Creeks or a slave of her former owners. Bob went to her and found out that the boy's name was Lyncoya.

Bob did not want to leave. He had convinced himself that he really should be at this last battle. It was God's will. After this one, the Cumberland Settlement would know the peaceful place they thought they were going to in '79. He was south of the Tennessee River, and crossing that body of water brought back memories of his journey to Nashville. He had fought Indians all the way. He had survived when many others hadn't. His courage and skill had saved the lives of many. It came to him that he might be the only person present who made the journey with the Donelson party. But, Andrew Jackson wanted him to take another saved child to Nashville. Rachel would have another child to dote on. What was it Miss Olive used to say? "The

Lawd works in mysterious ways." "He sho' do," agreed Bob, "but, you would think, just once, He'd mention it to Ole Bob first."

VI

Bob and Lyncoya left on a wagon in the company of several wounded men and the officer carrying dispatches. They carried only their bedrolls, Bob's cooking equipment, some dried meat, and several jugs containing water. They went to Huntsville. All the wounded survived the journey. Bob had tended to their needs, providing water and making them as comfortable as possible. Upon arrival, wounded were taken to a cabin, where they would receive what medical attention was available. To Bob's chagrin, the dispatch officer announced that he was leaving them behind. "You and that heathen brat slow me down too much," he barked. "I have lost too much time already. These dispatches must reach the Governor as soon as possible."

Bob protested, "Gen'ral Jackson say we to go with you. You know no black man can travel not escorted, 'specially with this Indian boy." Bob had left Nashville with the militia, so he did not think it necessary to bring proof of being a freeman.

"I've done what the General ordered. You have been delivered to safety. I'll inform the General's wife where you can be found when I deliver her letter." With that, he was off at a gallop.

Bob pondered their circumstances. At best, it would be a week before anybody came. The wagon and horses were the property of the army, so he was without transportation. If only he had thought to drive the wagon, he could claim it and go on his way. No, he thought, the Gen'ral should have said that the wagon be Bob's. Gen'ral Jackson gave him a few coins to purchase food, and he had some of his own. He hoped it would be enough to feed them. The most direct way to Nashville would be due north, the same route the militia had used. Bob reasoned that he did not know anybody along the way. He would be stopped and questioned by every sheriff and magistrate. He was already weary of being stopped in Huntsville and explaining who he was and why an Indian child was tagging after him. He could probably reach the Natchez Trace in two days if the boy could keep up. People on the Trace knew him, for he had traveled it many times. Maybe they could get a ride on a wagon. But, there were murderers and thieves on the Trace. He couldn't prove he was a freeman, and he couldn't prove Gen'ral Jackson sent him. He and the boy could end up dead, or worse yet, as slaves. But still, on the Trace, there were respected white folks who could confirm that he was indeed, Black Bob Renfro, a known tavern operator and freeman from Nashville. One thing did concern Bob more than all other obstacles: Winter was coming on. Bob rolled his eyes to the heavens, "Lawd, if this be one of your mysterious ways, I sho' do need some help."

Bob and Lyncoya stayed in Huntsville four more days before a part of his prayer was answered. A flatboat bound for Florence was coming apart and unloaded its cargo on the south side of the river. A driver was needed to haul supplies to *Pope's Tavern*. Bob and Lyncoya were aboard the wagon and crossing the river on the ferry before anybody could give it a second thought. They were traveling with another wagon, so Bob's fears of being stopped were somewhat relieved, even though he evaluated the other driver as shiftless trash. Still, he was a white man. His name was Clyde; Bob didn't know if that was his first or last name. It didn't make much difference. They hardly spoke, and all Bob needed to remember was to call him "Mister."

Mister Clyde started their eastward journey staying on the south side of the river. "Maybe he don't want no more of Huntsville either." As they pulled out, Bob looked down at the child, "Boy, ain't you ever gonna speak. What do you think 'bout this mess yo' new pa done got us in? I guess it be up to me to teach you white man civilized talk." Bob poked himself in the chest. "Uncle Bob," he pronounced. Then he poked the boy, "Lyncoya." The boy only nodded agreement.

The consignment was to be delivered to the inn just below and across the Shoals. As they crossed the river on *Colbert's Ferry*, Bob pointed upstream and explained, "That be where yo' Uncle Bob pulled Miss Rachel from the cold, cold water. Yes, suh, I saved yo' new ma's life. She was just a snip of a girl. A feisty little thing, though. Fell right off Capt'n Donelson's boat tryin' to help. Ole Bob see'd her fall. Master Renfro's boat was next in line. Miss Rachel was a calm one. She be bobbin' up and down with her arm stuck up in the air. I just plucked her from the water with one hand and never missed a stroke with my pole. Mistress Renfro wrapped her in a warm blanket. She was back with her ma and pa that night. Her pa was our leader. You never saw such a prideful, stubborn man. He never said a word to me, though I know'd he be happy I done what I done. Miss Rachel never forgit Ole Bob. That be why she told me 'bout Moses and showed me the letters so I could do a little readin'. She gonna teach you to read and write. I 'spect you be a proper gen'leman in time."

Bob's story was interrupted. "What the hell you doing with that boy?" George Colbert challenged. Colbert was a mixed-blood Chickasaw. He did not like the idea of an Indian child in the possession of a black man. During the crossing, Bob painstakingly explained his situation. The invocation of Gen'ral Jackson's name helped, but if Clyde hadn't chimed in with, "He's telling the truth," Bob hated to think about what would have happened next. He changed his opinion of Mister Clyde and would make a point of thanking him when they arrived at their destination.

"You tell your Gen'ral Jackson that just 'cause he's Indian, don't make him a house pet to be played with. That boy was meant to be a warrior," Colbert called after them, still unsure if he shouldn't intervene.

Pope's Tavern had been operating only two years. They did not know Bob. Though, they had heard stories about the black tavern owner in Nashville, especially about his gifted storytelling and cooking. Mister Pope didn't like the idea of a "free black and a young savage" being about his place. It might hurt business, and he certainly didn't want his slaves talking to him. He was, however, thankful to receive his supplies, so he allowed Bob and Lyncoya to sleep in the stable as partial payment for the delivery. He did not offer to feed them, so Bob used some of his funds to purchase a meal to be eaten outside. Clyde ate and slept in the tavern. Bob was able to catch him alone on his way back from the outhouse. "Mister Clyde, I sho' do want to thank you for speakin' up for me. I fear'd that man was gonna throw Ole Bob in the river."

"Colbert is low-life scum," responded Clyde and continued into the tavern.

Bob thought, "Just goes to show you can't tell a man's character just by lookin' at 'em." He didn't know for sure if he meant Clyde or Colbert or both.

As Bob settled his young charge down for the night, he pointed to various items around the stable and spoke their names: "horse," "cow," "chicken," "egg." Lyncoya gazed at Bob, closed his eyes and fell fast asleep. Bob was certain the boy could speak. He heard him chattering in his sleep. "Well, I reckon you just don't have nothin' to say just yet," deduced Bob as he closed his heavy eyes.

VII

They awoke early the next morning. Bob gathered half-a-dozen eggs, boiled them, and tucked them carefully away in his bedroll. They left before the people in the inn were awake, walking northwest in the direction of the Trace. At times Lyncoya walked beside Bob; at other times, something would catch his interest, and he would run ahead; still other times, Bob would lift the fatigued youngster to his shoulders. Bob knew from long experience not to get in a hurry. Neither the boy nor the pot got too heavy for him. They rested when the urge came upon them. As they walked, he was always alert for plants they could eat. Lyncoya had been raised in the wilderness, so he occasionally pointed to eatable berries and nuts that the frost or animals had missed. Bob praised the boy each time. Lyncoya's only acknowledgement was to nod. By nightfall, they were camping along the Natchez Trace and stewing a rabbit.

Several times they heard travelers along the way and hid in the underbrush. Lyncoya reveled in this game. Bob was thankful for the boy's silence. The third day, they heard a wagon approaching from the south. As soon as Bob saw that a black man was driving, he revealed himself.

The driver pulled up his team, "Who you be and what dat behin' you?" The driver of the wagon was not as dark-skinned as Bob, slightly larger than he, and at least twenty years younger. Bob decided that the formal approach was best, "I am called Robert Renfro, and this boy belongs to Gen'ral Andrew Jackson. I am takin' him to Gen'ral Jackson's home in Tennessee. Who are you and where are you goin'?"

"Well, ain't you the uppity one. I be ridin'. You be walkin' and you be talkin' mighty strong."

Bob decided on a change of tactics, "I 'poligize for any offense. I be called Bob, and I am in truth takin' this boy to Gen'ral Jackson's wife.

"Dat be better. You already in Tennessee. I be Henry, Masser Gene B. Harvey's man. I be takin' this here new wagon to 'em ner Columbia. I hear'ed of Gen'ral Jackson. Der be lots of talk 'bout 'em fightin' injuns. Ain't dat boy injun?"

"It be a long story. It getting' close to suppertime. What say we make camp together. I'll make us some supper, and we swap stories. You got a rifle?"

"Course I got a rifle. I a good shot too."

"Well, whiles it still be light, let's hunt us some fresh meat."

Darkness found Henry, Bob, and Lyncoya feasting on strips of fresh venison roasting before the fire. There would be enough to last for days. Bob prepared his pot. He selected several rounded rocks from the creek and placed them in the bottom, half covering them with water. He added some herbs and placed the pot in the coals. After the pot began to steam, he added a roast that he had near the fire. It had turned slightly brown. He placed the cover on the pot. "You just wait 'til mornin'. You taste somethin' then. We need to keep hot coals 'round the pot, not fire now, just coals. When one of us wakes up, put some more coals 'round the pot and add a little wood to the fire to make more coals. Gen'ral Jackson tell ever'body I the best camp cook he ever saw."

"Tell me 'bout dis boy," Henry said, and the swapping of stories began until they all fell asleep. Coals were added throughout the night, and morning arrived with much anticipation.

"I didn't know meat could be so tender 'less you pound it," Henry said between bites. "I thought you be crazy when you start to cook dem rocks."

"The rocks were just to keep the meat out of the water. Cook it slow and let the steam do the work. Most folks in too big a hurry. If'n you got some bread, the drippin's is good too, or you can start a good stew."

"I done clean fergit. I got a poke full of cornpones." The three of them sopped the warm gravy, lay back, and thought, "Life don't get better than this."

Henry broke the spell, declaring, "We best break camp 'n git started. You be 'bout fifty miles from Nashville when we gits to Columbia. I 'spect we got two mo' days travelin' 'n eatin' yo' cookin'. You say you was in Huntsville goin' to Nashville, 'n now you way over here. Dat don't make good sense."

"It be what Gen'ral Jackson would call a slight miscalculation. It be a long story."

"We gots time."

They continued to trade stories. Henry was a trusted man. He came and went on his own schedule. Master Harvey knew he would come back after he finished his assigned task. He could be trusted with money too. He

204

had papers with him to prove that his master had sent him on this trip. Henry confessed to Bob that he had heard of him.

"Hellfire, Bob, ever' black man in Tennessee hear'ed of you. You come here a slave, you saved yo' massa's wife and chill'un from injuns after dey done kilt 'em, 'n now you be a freeman with yo' own biz'nez. You good as any white man."

"Don't say that too loud, Henry. Whites got a way of thinkin' that don't allow that. You take even Gen'ral Jackson. I done as much for that man as Judge John Overton and Gen'ral John Coffee. Him and Miss Rachel calls me Uncle now. That be as much respect as white folks can show. To be fair now, I never made Ole Andy no big money, 'cept one time he bet on a horse. Them others always involved in some big land deal. They use to sit in my backroom and plot their next doin's. They never tried to keep secrets from me. To this day, I don't know if it was trust or they thought a black man just plain too stupid to take advantage. I made a few dollars off of what I hear'ed them say. But a black man has to be careful not to make too much at one time."

They traveled on at a slow but steady pace, stopping when the horses needed rest. They stopped at the places where Bob was known. Henry purchased feed for the horses, and Bob purchased some potatoes and onions. "This'll eat right where you hold it," Bob said. Bob's nonsense sayings were seldom questioned. They seemed to have a meaning that anyone should understand.

Lyncoya found the bed of the wagon to be perfect. He created his own world with bedrolls and equipment, joyfully played, and rested throughout the day. After one such stop, Bob playfully tossed Lyncoya upon one of the horses. He seemed to like it until Bob started away. The boy was quickly down and in the wagon. "Dat boy want you so he can see youse," said Henry.

It was Lyncoya that spotted the critter. He jumped from the wagon, picked up a stick, and attacked the ugly varmint. It appeared to be dead. "It only playin' dead. Now I shows you some real cookin'. This here 'possum gonna be so tasty you think you be dead and done gone to he'ven," Bob prophesized.

"I be thinkin'. When I first see'd you 'n de boy, you say yo' name Robert. den you say it be Bob. How dat be?" quizzed Henry.

"It's a long story."

"We gots time."

Bob and Henry lapsed into easy bantering and casual talk, two black men enjoying their time alone, isolated from the rest of the world. They particularly enjoyed using familiar names for white men. Mister and Master were dropped; they became Old Man So and So. They knew well enough that this time was short and reality would set in at the sight of the first white man, but with winter coming on there were not many travelers on the Trace. Henry only had to show his papers once.

They passed *Grinder's Stand* about midday, but did not stop. "Bad things happen dar. Som'body 'portant got kilt," whispered Henry.

"I know 'bout it. There be talk in my tavern. It was Gov'nor Mer'weatha Lewis. He be Gov'nor of all the land the other side of the Mississippi River. Him and some man named Clark explored the terr'tory.

Gen'ral Jackson say he was a friend of Pres'dent Thomas Jefferson. Gen'ral Jackson knows all them folks. Them Grinders said he shot himself. Gen'ral Jackson say they murdered him, and they ought to hang for it, the old woman too. He say ain't no man shoots himself in the side and in the head."

It took a day longer to reach their destination than expected. Henry had to have one more night of what he thought must be the best of times. When they reached the turn-off to Columbia, Henry persuaded Bob to continue into town. "Master Harvey be a good man; he be proud to send word to Missus Jackson, 'n she send som'body to git you and de boy. Ain't ever'body in Columbia can say dey done Gen'ral Andrew Jackson a favor. I wants my woman Ophelia to know I done met Bob Renfro, 'n if'n you don't mind, dat I calls him friend. 'Sides, I thinks snow be in the air."

"Henry, I be proud to call you friend. To tell you the truth, I don't know many black men well enough to call them friend. And you right about that snow."

After Master Harvey heard Henry's explanation, he shouted, "By thunder, I'll do better than that. I'll send a rider to Mistress Jackson, and as soon as this snow lets up, I'll take you myself. You come, too, Henry. I've got business in Nashville. Take them to your cabin for now." During the night, it started to snow harder. It was most of a week before the snow let up.

VII

Bob stayed in Henry's cabin, along with Ophelia and four children. Lyncoya played with the children. By now, it was everyone's mission to get the boy to speak. But he did not. "Jist ain't gots nuffin' to say. Dat all der be to it. Dat child be smart as dey comes. When he got sump'in to say, you hear it," Ophelia offered her opinion with the knowing ways of a mother.

Bob showed Ophelia some of his cooking secrets, and she shared hers. The remainder of the deer meat was still good because of the weather having been so cold. Ophelia fixed squirrel and corn in a stew that Bob declared was "fit for the table of Gen'ral Andrew Jackson, himself." Bob decided when he left, he would leave the cooking pot with Ophelia.

"Bob, you gots a woman?" Ophelia asked.

"No, m'am, I ain't. Never found one that would have me," he smiled.

"I knows dat ain't true. You's a fine lookin' man. You got money. Must be sump'in else."

Bob did not want to tell Ophelia his opinion of producing children to be field hands for white masters. After a long pause he said, "To tell you the truth, when I first come here, ain't no colored women to speak of—just men to help with the crops. Gen'ral Jackson had a girl I liked just fine, but before I knows her good, she up and died."

Bob drifted off into another world as he stared into the fire. Then he continued, "There was a woman once. Met her down in New Orleans.

Her name was Janette. She was a pretty little thing. She was a freewoman too. I saw her on a couple of my trips. But, she said she wouldn't come to Tennessee, and I wouldn't leave. She married another man. Broke my heart, don't you know?" Bob had never mentioned Janette to anyone before. Being with a family made him nostalgic for what might have been.

Ophelia studied Bob and Lyncoya for a while; then she could contain herself no longer, she asked what was on her mind. "Bob, what gonna happen with dat boy? Henry try to 'splain. It still not clear to me"

"I tell you honest, I don't know," Bob confessed. "The Gen'ral say 'raise the little heathen in the house."

"Will he be slave or free?"

"Don't know. White folks don't usually make slaves of injuns. Other injuns do, but white folks don't."

Henry joined the conversation: "That be som'thing I wants to know 'bout. We all quick 'nough to kill 'em, seem to me dey be mo' use as slaves."

Bob could not pass up the opportunity to pontificate on the subject. "Years ago Gen'ral Jackson and Miss Rachel both try to 'splain slavery to me," he started, and when he was sure he had their undivided attention, he continued. "But you know that learned men from the college frequent my establishment, so hear'd many a discussion on the subject. Some consider injuns to be too stupid to be fit slaves. They say that after hundreds of years injuns still don't understand the wheel; they still drag their belongings tied on to sticks. One man say the Spanish tried to make slaves of 'em to find gold. But it broke the men's spirits and they just died. They married up with the injun women though. Lots of children. Don't try to make sense of it. My head hurts sometimes when I think too much on why white people do things."

He observed his audience of two were wide-eyed. They had not noticed that his speech pattern had changed, so he went on, "Now you take them Cherokees the Gen'ral done got friendly with. After all the fighting over all the years, they becoming just like whites. They farming, they buying black slaves, and they building churches—becoming *civilized* it's called. But down in New Orleans free black men doing the same thing, buying black slaves I mean."

This was too much for Henry. He interrupted, "You say der be black men who own other black men?" How do they d'cide who be free 'n who be slave?"

"It be complicated," Bob acknowledged and resumed his lecture, "These learned men that come to my place, they say the Romans, they was before the Spanish, make slaves of everybody they beat in war. Don't make no difference what color yo' skin; you lose—you be a slave. In the Bible just about everybody have slaves, 'cept Jesus. Egypt people get to make all Jews slaves 'til Moses say, 'Let my people go!' Then somehow dem Romans make Jews slaves again. There is just slaves everywhere. They say it's the natural order of things."

"De nat'ral orda?" quizzed Ophelia.

"That's kinda what they say when they wants God to take the blame for what they doing," Bob answered.

Henry's eyes had closed and Ophelia was wondering just who these Spanish and Romans were; but it was late, so she gently nudged Henry's outstretched barefoot and declared, "It be time fer bed. Full day o' work 'morrow."

Lyncoya was asleep in a pile of little black bodies. Ophelia covered them all with a quilt. Henry banked the fire. Bob decide he would spend this night in the barn. With a nod, he bid them a good night and concluded, "Like I say sometimes it makes my head hurt to think so much on it."

After Bob had gotten comfortable he began to think about his lecture on slavery. "I should of told them more. Professor Hubbard use to talk about white slaves. Said the English make slaves of the Irish and there's some people called *serfs* that are slaves all over Europe. Rich people makes them work the land. And there was somethin' 'bout white people who make a contract to be rich folks' slaves, *indentured servants* he called them. I don't see why nobody would agree to be a slave if'n they had a choice. I wished I hadn't started thinking on this. For sure, my head's gonna hurt a long time." Bob rolled onto his side and stared into the darkness until he went to sleep.

Columbia was on the route between Nashville and General Jackson's army. Mister Harvey generously passed on news while Bob was helping out with the chores. Bob could not help but smile when he heard that the Gen'eral's stomach had gotten out of sorts almost immediately after he left. Bob felt some vindication for having been sent away. General Jackson had to contend with militia enlistments ending and insufficient food for the army. There were still frequent encounters with small Indian parties. The conclusion was that Jackson had bit off more than he could chew, but was too stubborn to give it up.

Bob confided in Henry, "He went there to put an end to it. He will stay there as long as it takes. Even if he be the only one left to fight. He will win, or he will be dead."

Mister Harvey informed Henry that the way to Nashville was passable and that they would leave the next morning. The message to Rachel Jackson had been sent with the dispatch rider who stopped by to water his horse. They left well before daylight with the intention of making the Hermitage in one day. Mister Harvey would go directly to Nashville. He felt that taking care of Jackson's Indian and Bob for over a week had established the debt if he ever needed a favor from the General.

Bob felt a pain in his chest when he spotted the two-story cabin where Miss Rachel lived. Bob asked Henry to stop the wagon. He took Lyncoya and placed him astride a horse again. "No reason why you shouldn't git here lookin' like a warrior." Lyncoya sensed the importance of the moment and raised himself to his full height, something he had not done since General Jackson's tent.

As the wagon approached, Rachel and Little Andrew came out to the front. "At long last," she said, holding back tears of joy. "I've been so worried about you. Nobody seemed to know where you were. And then Mister Harvey's message came."

"Is that my Indian? The one Papa sent me?" demanded Little Andrew.

"Hush, child. Give Uncle Bob time to catch his breath."

"Lyncoya don't talk much, Miss Rachel. Matter of fact he ain't said a word in the whole month I knowed him. But he a smart boy. I be proud to have him for my son."

"Come here, child." Her soft voice seemed to calm the little warrior, who had suddenly clung to Bob's leg.

"You go on now, boy. This be your new ma."

"He don't look like much," said Andrew. "He's so little." Bob knew instinctively that young Mister Jackson was going to be a problem. So did Lyncoya.

Rachel took Lyncoya's hand and tried to reassure him. "Do you know what his name means?" she questioned.

"No m'am, I clean forgit to ask." He hesitated, then added as he climbed up next to Henry. "I got to be gettin' in to town. You send word if'n you wants me."

Just as Henry gave the command to start the horses, Lyncoya received a sharp blow from his new companion. "Unkie Bob, Unkie Bob," the child cried his first words as Rachel tightened her grip on his wrist.

"Keep drivin'!" Tears streamed down Bob's face. "Now I remembers what it be like to be slave. Ain't nothin' I can do. Ain't nothin' nobody can do. Keep drivin' and don't look back."

Bob left another part of his heart at the Hermitage that day. He had grown to love that little boy so. He had been a father for a month.

THIRTEEN
FIRE!

Bob was following his usual routine on Friday night. He had supervised the cooking and serving of the evening meal and then had joined his guests for a pipe of tobacco and a glass of imported Madeira wine. The conversation had centered around the actions of the Tennessee General Assembly, which had been meeting in Nashville, the progress of the war with Great Britain, and the movements of their militia still campaigning against Creeks in the South. They accepted Bob's evaluation that General Jackson would not return to Tennessee until total victory was achieved. "He'll come back here a'ridin' that big white horse at the head of his army with all flags a'flyin', else he be dead," Bob proclaimed to one and all. About 9 o'clock the guests in residence started drifting off to their rooms and the locals left for their homes. Saturday would be just another workday, so they needed their rest. Bob gave instructions to Elisha to make sure their guests' needs were attended to and to see to their horses.

"Just who does Mister Bob think took care of business while he was off with the Gen'ral," Elisha thought to himself. "He taught me ever'thing there is to know 'bout operatin' a tavern. Had me taught to read and write and work with numbers, but he's still the boss and the closest thing to a pa I ever had. So, we'll do it your way, Mister Robert Renfro."

Bob stepped out on to the night streets of Nashville. The full moon had just started to wane so there was ample light for a short stroll. He noticed a slight breeze and then took a deep breath. "That smells like smoke," he thought, seconds before he heard a man yell, "Fire! Fire! Fire!"

"That looks like that good-for-nothin' Terrell," he said out loud. Then he noticed the sky; flames and smoke were shooting out of a warehouse just down the street. He ran back into the tavern. "Elisha! Elisha! Get ever'body up and get'em out of here! The whole place is on fire!"

Bob and Elisha ran about the tavern shouting, rousing, and informing their guests. Next they headed for the stables and led the horses to safety. They then returned to the site of the fire, which was raging out of control. "Mister Bob, we ain't gonna put that fire out with buckets of water."

Bob's shoulders slumped as he surrendered with a heavy heart.

"It just got too much of a start," Elisha consoled.

"You are right 'bout that. All of Nashville might go up in smoke 'fore this night be over. Check and make sure all of our customers are safe. I see most of 'em with buckets in that line. I done got my box of import'nt papers and the money that was in the place."

"Yes, suh. Mister Bob, I saved your banjo and two kegs of yo' sippin' whiskey. If'n that fire reaches the mixin' room, there is gonna be a terrible explosion."

"Ain't no if'n—it be when."

THE DEMOCRATIC CLARION & TENNESSEE GAZETTE
NASHVILLE
TUESDAY — MARCH 15,
Dreadful Fire!!!

Under the dispensation of divine providence, we have again to record the destructive effects of this ungovernable element—-

On Friday night last, about 10 o'clock, the citizens of this town were alarmed with the cry of fire! It proceeded from the hay-loft of Wm. W. Cook, Esq. near Mr. Woods warehouse; it had gained such an ascendency & the buildings were so combustible, that the utmost exertions of the citizens could not save the large adjoining warehouse, filled with consignments to Joseph Wood, esq. commission merchant, the bindery, dwelling house and bookstore of Mr. Duncan Robertson, the tavern house of Robert Rentfroe, the frame house of John Anderson esq, the house occupied by Mr. Ernest Beniot, baker, the shop of Messrs. E. and G. Hewlett saddlers above; the dwelling house of Wm. W. Cooke esq, the dwelling house occupied by Mr. S. V. Stout, the warehouse of Messrs, Reed and Washington, army contractors, and their office, the shop & dwelling house of Mr. D. C. Snow, tin plate worker, below; the dwelling house of Joseph T. Elliston, and his silversmith shop, the dwelling house of the editor of the Clarion & his printing office, the house lately occupied by Wm M. Wallace, as a shoemaker's shop and the house occupied by Joseph Sumner, the property of Mr. John Young, the office of the Nashville Whig and the hatter's shop of Mr. Joshua Pilcher, and the brick store house occupied by V. Tannehill, esq. above, on the east side of Market street, & all the frame building on the same side opposite to bank alley, making in the whole the most destructive fire experienced in the western country. No language can paint the distress of many of the suffers, who left without bread; meat, dishes or plates, or a covering except the heavens. In the whole range of the fire we are however gratified that no lives were lost, and we hope that in a few years a majority of the sufferers will be able to replace the property they have thus lost. In some few cases we are, however, sorry to learn the individuals are ruined. It is impossible at present, to form an estimate of the immense loss sustained—nearly one half the buildings that were in the town are in ashes; much furniture and other valuable property was lost in the flames. Among the sufferers, the Editor of this Paper finds it necessary to repeat that he was one —- his Printing Office contained many printed books and pamphlets, the most of which were lost, and he is sorry to state, in that situation is the Journal of the proceedings of the last General Assembly, which was nearly entirely lost. Of the Journals of the house of Representatives, it is believed a copy can be made out; but of the Senate there is not the least hope of ever recovering one, for the printing and manuscript shared the same fate. Of the heavy additions of the heavy editions of law books, &e, &e, in the house, it is believed scarcely a copy remains: and of the printing apparains, a considerable part was lost; but one press and nearly all the type was saved. For the satisfaction of the members of the last General Assembly, he is thus particular that the loss of the public Journals may be rightly understood.

The fire was communicated, we have little doubt, by some incendiary —who is not yet ascertained

II

Bob was saddened. But, he was thankful that all of his friends and customers were still alive. He had attended the Reverend Craighead's prayer service with them. Most of the things he had accumulated were gone. He now knew how Miss Olive felt after she lost everything. She went on though—taking it as the "Lord's mysterious ways." He would have to do the same. Miss Rachel had sent word that if there was anything he needed to let her know. He was lost in his thoughts when he heard a despondent Elisha ask, "Mister Bob, what we gonna do? Ever'thing you own is gone."

"Do? I don't know for sure. I got the money to rebuild if'n I wants too. My credit's good anywhere in Nashville if'n I need more. We got our papers. First thing is to make sure ever'body that rented from us has a place to stay and all the people who worked for us got enough to get by on. People gonna stand in line for buildin' materials. This time we build it all out of bricks."

Only ten days passed before there were notices published in *The Gazette* and *The Tennessee Whig:*

ROBERT RENFRO

HAVING, in common with many others, had his house burnt down in the late destructive fire, and having since rented the stone tavern on the public square, near the court-house, informs his friends, former customers, and the public in general, that he will continue his public house in that building. He does not intend retailing spirits to country customers; and will endeavor to preserve the same order in the house that he formerly has done. A few decent boarders would be taken. Those who call will find attention paid to their convenience.
March 22.   82-tf.

217

The first former tenant to call on Bob was James Powers, who worked for the army contractors. "Well, Bob its good to know I'll have you feeding me and looking out for me again. How did you arrange this so fast?" he asked.

"Why Mister Jim, I look out for all my friends, and as to how I done it, all I gots to say is, 'This ain't no step for a high stepper like Ole Black Bob Renfro.'"

FOURTEEN
LOOKING BACK – 1819

Bob Renfro sat on the bluff overlooking the Cumberland River at Nashville, just above the original settlement. Across the river was the land James Shaw had owned. Signs of the coming of spring were all about him. Some early flowering trees were budding and a few ground plants were in bloom. March 11, 1819, was still cool, but the bright sun made it pleasant to be outside. Bob's eyesight was not what it used to be. He could still see the big print in the newspaper, but the stories had to be interpreted by Elisha. Looking down the river toward the big bend had become his greatest joy. "Just sittin' and thinkin' 'bout nothin'," he called it. He was gazing at the newest wonderment: a steamboat named the *General Jackson*. "Billy Carroll done pulled one off this time. If'n we'd had his boat in '79, things sho' would have been differ'nt. That old boat of Cap'n Donelson's, I thought was so big. Well, it was big, big as Noah's Ark, for all I knowed; it took 'bout thirty men and Mistress Ann Johnston on the tiller when they poled it upstream. They tells me that this boat came from New Orleans in less time than it took us to get from the mouth of this river to Red Paint Hill. It can travel when the water high, and it can travel when the water low, long as there ain't no rapids. They could even go to Pittsburgh, if'n they wants. I might just get on it and go to Pittsburgh. I sho' bought a lot of goods that come from there, but I never been there. For all it can do, that boat can't go where we went. It can't do no Muscle Shoals. We still King of the River!" His chest swelled a little with his last thought.

He hadn't shown much spunk since he got back from his trip with the militia and then the fire, just five years ago today. His hair had turned completely white. Now, even strangers called him "Uncle" because of his age and dignified appearance. He went to the Hermitage once with some made-up excuse when what he really wanted was to see Lyncoya. He saw the boy, but there was not much between them. "I knows you thinks I betrayed you, but you got to understand, boy, you belongs to Miss Rachel. I just brung you here like the Gen'ral say. I sho' do hope when you grows up you understand. I hopes the Lawd work less mysterious ways on you."

Henry came up occasionally from Columbia to pick up supplies for Master Harvey and stayed the night with Bob. Their journey on the Natchez Trace was never discussed. Henry had seen Bob cry, and men did not discuss those times. October was Henry's last visit. They had sat before the fire smoking pipes and enjoying Bob's special sippin' whiskey. Bob's special libation had a way of turning men into deep thinkers and philosophers.

Henry said, "Youse knows what yo tribe be?"

"Tribe...? What you mean?"

"Well, it seems to me when black men gits together dey starts tryin' to figger out de Africa tribe dey be from."

"Africa tribe? I don't even know where Africa is or how to get there. I don't even know where the ocean is 'cept go east a long long way, and then Africa som'where on the other side. If'n you gets on the river out here and just starts floatin', you can go all the way to New Orleans. You can find a ocean, but it won't even be the right ocean."

"Don't youse wants to know?"

"I tell you this: After all I been through, I think I be as much a part of Tennessee and this country as Gen'ral Andrew Jackson himself."

"I guess it be diff'rent fer a freeman."

"I tell you somethin' else on that subject. Black people ain't ever goin' to be free as long as they ignorant. We all got to learn to read and write. Just look at how much I knows that ain't gonna be passed on 'cause I can't write it down. I can read a little writin' but I can't write no readin'." Both men appreciated the humor and the wisdom in this remark. They pondered it as Bob poured each just a little more of the wonderful liquid in the jug. Bob continued his dissertation, "Spizzerinctum, that's the thing. Ain't nobody gonna give it to you—You can't buy it. The spizz'—You gotta do that yo'self." He paused for Henry's comment, but nothing came. So, he continued, "You know, Henry, white folks makes a record of ever'thin' they do. They gots their Bible, that be a record that happened a long long time ago. I gettin' old, ain't gonna be here much longer, but a hun'red years from now folks can go to the white man's records and it will say Ole Bob was made a freeman by the State of Tennessee. They can find 'bout me goin' to court with Mister Dickinson and Gen'ral Jackson shootin' him. It all be in the record. I been ponderin' 'bout it for lots of years. Just what makes white folks think it be proper to take red men's land and treat black men like property? It be 'cause we ain't got no records. It ain't wrote down nowhere."

221

All the weighty conclusions Bob had reached over the years came pouring out of him. "And they gots the rule of law. The Bible be full of laws and rules to live by. My Mistress, Miss Olive, she liked to use the law when she thought she had been wronged. Mister Searcy and the Gen'ral was always saying…" Bob rose to his feet, placed his hand on his chest gripping his shirt and assumed his most dignified stance and voice, " 'To be a civilized nation we must always follow the rule of law.'"

Henry smiled at the performance.

"I used the rule of law just recently when I had that trouble with that bogtrotter Richardson Tyre and his mean spiteful wife Rose. Crazy woman is agin drinkin' and playin' cards. Come right in my own place, called me names and attack me. I didn't do nuth'in but get me a lawyer and took 'em to court. Had two cases. One on him and one on both of 'em. Won 'em too. A jury of white men say they was guilty of trespass and assault. Strange thing though, the court only gave me one cent in each case. So I got two cents and they had to pay the court fees. But, like my lawyer say, I didn't get compensation but I got satisfaction and justice. That be important under the rule of law. I had that old bogtrotter John Boyd before the court too. He cut up my tables when he was drunk and in a rage. He had to pay for 'em, a hundred dollars. You see Henry, I be more than a freeman. I own property and I pay taxes. That be impor'ant too."

Henry interrupted Bob's presentation with the only question he could think of, "What be a bogtrotter?"

"Oh, that's what Mister Bradford over at the newspaper calls people that makes him mad."

After a brief timeout, Bob decided to make one more point, "I don't understand all I knows about them Masons. Mister Jim Powers is one of 'em. He told me a little bit, and sometimes they met in my backroom. They calls themselves the Free and Accepted Masons. They stick together on most things and he'p each other out. Gen'ral Jackson, Gov'nor Roane, the Searcy brothers, they all be Masons. I hear'd Pres'dent Washington be one too. A lot of it be secret with fancy titles and they calls each other 'Brother.' They was gittin' organized here 'bout the time I got my freedom. I just wonder if them he'pin' each other out, he'ped me out. I wouldn't mind being a Mason myself—I'm free and accepted by most folks."

The conversation had long ago gone beyond Henry's comprehension. He changed the subject. "Youse see dat injun boy lately?"

"Only once to talk to. He just kind of looked at me all bewildered like."

"Well, what youse 'spect. He jist a baby. He done seen his folks kilt. Den yo hatchet-face beanpole of a gen'ral snatches him up and sends him packin' with a black man. 'Bout de time he gits to trust ye, youse gives him to Miss Rachel, and dat boy o' hers pops 'em upside the head 'fore we can even git gone. Youse be bewildered too." Henry had summed it up as well as it could be done. "Maybe he gits over it. Maybe he don't." They got lost in their thoughts and dozed off contented from the warmth of the fire, mellowed by their drink, and at ease in their friendship.

Bob had seen Lyncoya from a distance a few times in a carriage with Miss Rachel. Lyncoya was dressed just like young Andrew. He didn't look very comfortable; it caused Bob that same pain he felt when he arrived at the Hermitage, knowing he and the boy would part. Bob kept hoping Miss Rachel would send for him again. The message never came. He figured she was busy running that big farm while the Gen'ral was off fighting. But, then, too, Miss Rachel seemed to have changed some, "taking on airs," as he had heard some white ladies say. From all the things Bob had heard and from what Elisha told him was in the newspaper, Miss Rachel and the Gen'ral had a right to be mighty proud.

Bob started running the last few years through his mind: "Gen'ral Andrew Jackson and his Tennessee Militia and them orn'ry redskins he got friendly with had whooped them Creeks at a place called Horseshoe Bend. For some reason, the Gen'ral did not hang Weartherford like he said he was. Then he got himself to be a big gen'ral in the whole United States Army. Billy Carroll then get to be the Tennessee gen'ral. Let me see what happened next. I heared som'thin' 'bout Florida, and then he go to New Orleans and give them British a proper whoppin'. He was gonna fight them once before. That's when all that stuff at Natchez happened, and he come home powerful mad. Then them Benton brothers near kilt him; then the Creek mess and Lyncoya. I thinks I got it all straight. How can one man get into so much? That New Orleans must have been the biggest fight ever. They celebrated here in Nashville for a week, and Miss Rachel went off down to New Orleans so as she could party with the Gen'ral. They come back to Nashville for a little while; then goes off to Washington for a parade. The whole country wants to see him. They went back off to Florida again. I guess he just too busy to see Ole Uncle Bob. He send Ole Sam by som'times to make sure I all right. There is talk 'bout Andrew Jackson ought to be pres'dent. I ain't too sure 'bout that. I heared Gen'ral Jackson talk bad about all the pres'dents. He don't cut no slack to George Washin'ton and Thomas Jeffe'son and now Mr. Madison. I heared him sit in my back room and call them all scoundrels and fools. Why if'n the Gen'ral heared they'd talked that way 'bout him, he say, 'Get yo' pistol. We goin' to Kentuck. We settle this right now.' Why would he wants to be pres'dent? Long time ago he got 'lected to Congress; I believe that was '96. Next year they made him Senator. He didn't stay long either time; he rather be Judge. He don't like nobody up there. Heared him say so myself lots of times. Mostly he just likes bein' the Gen'ral."

Bob let the sun continue to warm his bones for a while longer. "I ought to get up from here and go...go where? I ain't got no place to go. I done let Elisha run the business. I thought the boy would be free som'day. But, times they are a changin'. The court told the Gen'ral he could free Ole Sam if'n Sam go back to Africa. Sam say he rather be a slave in Tennessee. I done sold 'bout ever'thing I ever had. I don't need no mo' money. The work it takes to make whiskey and cook proper just too much for me now." He chuckled to himself, "I just tells folks how to do it now. Ever'thing 'cept makin'sippin' whiskey. They should have watched me closer with them coals from cookin' fires. If'n I sits here, som'body will come by to talk with. I still spins the best tales in Tennessee. The white boys, when they ain't showin' off, likes to hear the stories 'bout the ole days. Whenever som'body wants to know 'how it use to be,' they say, 'Go ask Uncle Bob; he knows—he was there.' Yes, suh, I think I just sit here and watch Nashville grow."

EPILOGUE

A light snow was falling the first week in January 1829. The lean figure of Andrew Jackson, President-elect of the United States of America was making a final visit to Spring Hill Cemetery above a high bluff on the Cumberland River. He was dressed in his most formal military uniform. It was a solitary visit to a solitary grave. He had ordered that he be left alone with his thoughts.

He knew he wanted to say something, but the words would not come to him. He knew, too, that the words must and would convey something of importance. On the ride from the Hermitage, the words would start forming in his mind, but then he would dismiss them or they would just slip away. At long last, he removed his hat and fell to his knees speaking what was in his heart.

"Old friend, I could not come sooner. I should have come last spring when Lyncoya died. He had the consumption; he could not be saved. It has been only fourteen years since you took him from that battlefield. I know you loved that boy as if he were your own. Now we've lost our beloved Rachel too. We laid her to rest just last week. Her tender heart could take no more of the slings and arrows thrown by my opponents. There was a special bond between you two. I believe there is a heaven, and I believe that you three, who went through so much together, are receiving your just and eternal reward.

" I have been elected President. I know you do not think much of that. But I swear before God that I will do my best. The world will never know what you did to make all this come about. You saved both of our lives. I leave for Washington City soon. I have to leave behind so many that mean so much to me. The burden of knowing who are already in their graves is all a man can bear.

"When I came here this morning, I knew that there was something I must say. And I confess to you and Almighty God that it was difficult to come to. We have called you Uncle Bob these many years. What I want to say is…" The words seemed to get stuck in his throat. "What I want to say is…"

General Andrew Jackson rose to feet and replaced his hat; his back became ramrod straight; his right arm bent at the elbow; and his index finger came to rest on his forehead. He checked the tears welling in his eyes; then he spoke in a loud, clear voice, "I salute you, Robert Renfro. You were a gentleman."

APPENDIX

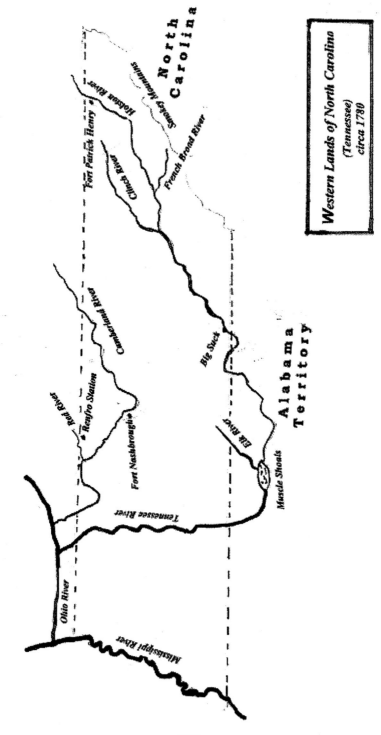

Western Lands of North Carolina
(Tennessee)
circa 1780

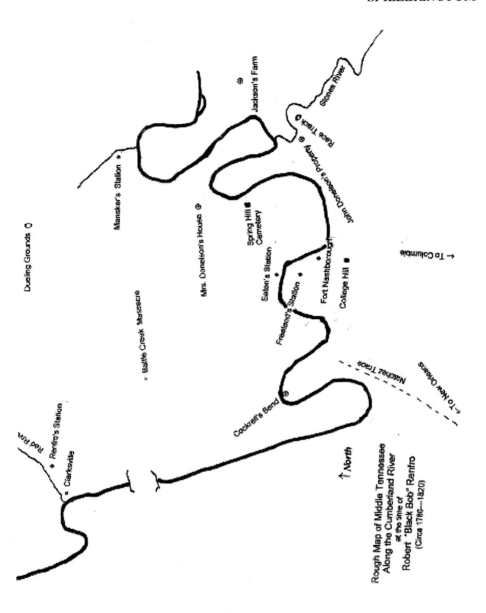

Rough Map of Middle Tennessee
Along the Cumberland River
at the time of
Robert "Black Bob" Renfro
(Circa 1780—1820)

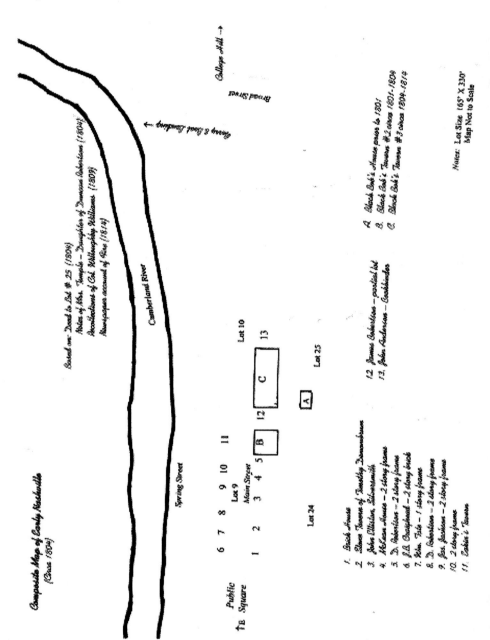

Composite Map of Early Nashville
(Circa 1804)

Based on: Deed to Lot # 25 (1804)
Notes of Mrs. Temple - Daughter of Duncan Robertson (1804)
Recollections of Col. Willoughby Williams (1809)
Newspaper account of fire (1814)

Gallops Hill →

Broad Street

← Stump's Boat Landing

Cumberland River

Notes: Lot Size 165' X 330'
Map Not to Scale

A. Black Bob's house prior to 1801
B. Black Bob's Tavern #2 circa 1801-1804
C. Black Bob's Tavern #3 circa 1804-1814

12. James Robertson – practical lot
13. John Anderson – Cabbinetter

Lot 10

13

C

Lot 25

12
A
B

Spring Street

Lot 9

Main Street

6 7 8 9 10 11
1 2 3 4 5

Lot 24

Public
B Square

1. Brick house
2. Stone Tavern of Timothy Demonbreun
3. John Elliston, Silversmith
4. McLean house – 2 story frame
5. D. Robertson – 2 story frame
6. J.D. Craighead – 2 story brick
7. Rhea, Yale – 1 story frame
8. D. Robertson – 2 story frame
9. Geo. Jackson – 2 story frame
10. 2 story frame
11. Cabin's Tavern

232

RESOURCES

The following are some of the books that aided me in my search for Black Bob. Various sites on the Internet provided much of the general information.

Robert H. White – *TENNESSEE - Its Growth and Progress*

Robert H. White – *MESSAGES OF THE GOVERNORS OF TENNESSEE 1796-1821, Volume One*

Marquis James — *ANDREW JACKSON – The Border Captain*

James W. Ely, Jr., Theodore Brown, Jr., editors — *LEGAL PAPERS OF ANDREW JACKSON*

Ursula Smith Beach — *ALONG THE WARIOTO – A History of Montgomery County, Tennessee*

Charles Waters — *HISTORIC CLARKSVILLE – The Bicentennial Story 1784-1984*

W. P. Titus – *PICTURESQUE CLARKSVILLE, PAST AND PRESENT A History of the City of Hills*

Thomas A. Bailey – *THE AMERICAN PAGENT – A History of the Republic*

Chase C. Mooney – *SLAVERY IN TENNESSEE*

Bobby L. Lovett – *THE AFRICAN-AMERICAN HISTORY OF NASHVILLE, TENNESSEE, 1780-1930*

Anita Shafer Goodstein – *NASHVILLE 1780–1860 – From Frontier to City*

Bethenia McLemore Oldam – *TENNESSEE...AND TENNESSEANS*

Larry Michael Ellis

G. R. McGee – *HISTORY OF TENNESSEE – From 1663 to 1900*

J. G. M. Ramsey, A.M., M.D. — *The ANNALS of TENNESSEE to the End of the Eighteenth Century*

The Goodspeed Publishing Company — *HISTORY of TENNESSEE - ILLUSTRATED*

A.W. Putman – *HISTORY OF MIDDLE TENNESSEE The Life and Times of General James Robertson*

Edward Albright – *EARLY HISTORY OF MIDDLE TENNESSEE*

E. Bushnell – *AN EARLY DISCRIPTION OF MIDDLE TENNESSEE*

Samuel Cole Williams – *TENNESSEE DURING THE REVOLUTIONARY WAR*

State of Tennessee – *ACTS PASSED AT THE FIRST SESSION OF THE FOURTH GENERAL ASSEMBLY OF THE STATE OF TENNESSEE*

State of Tennessee – *JOURNALS OF THE HOUSE OF REPRESENTATIVES AND SENATE AT THE* FIRST SESSIONOF THE FOURTH GENERAL ASSEMBLY

The Tennessee Historical Society – *THE TENNESSE ENCYCLOPEDIA of HISTORY & CULTURE*

The Tennessee Historical Society – *THREE TENNESSEE PIONEER DOCUMENTS*

Tennessee Secretary of State – *TENNESSEE BLUE BOOK*

Robert "Black Bob" Renfro – Documented

December 1779
Bob is the slave of Joseph and Olive Renfro. Joseph is a relative of Moses Renfro. The Renfros join John Donelson for the river voyage to the Cumberland Settlement in the western lands of North Carolina.

April 12, 1780 – *John Donelson's Journal*
Moses Renfro and party leave the Donelson party at the mouth of the Red River, site of present day Clarksville, Tennessee, travel upstream and establish Renfro Station.

June 1780
Joseph Renfro is killed in an Indian raid. Most Renfros make it to Fort Nashborough though it is unclear as to when and how they got there.

October 1786 – *Davidson County Court Minutes 1783-1792, p. 140*
Olive Shaw is granted letters of administration on the estate of Joseph Renfro, deceased.

July term 1793 – *Will Book I: Davidson County Jan. 1784-April 1794, p. 285*
Recorded Aug. 8, 1792, Bill of Sale: Shaw to Mays. Olive Shaw, John Renfro and Josiah Love, "for valuable consideration…sold 1 negro man named Bob…"

1793-94 — *Minutes of Superior Court of North Carolina including Mero District, p. 161*
A series of court cases between Robert Nelson and Josiah Love results in Bob being auctioned at a sheriff's sale. Robert Searcy is high bidder. However, Love had also sold Bob to Elijah Robertson. Searcy and Robertson agreed to submit the case to the Superior Court. Court decides Searcy is the rightful owner. Andrew Jackson lawyer for Love.

January 16, 1794 – *Minutes of the County Court of Davidson County* 1791-1797, Book "B", p. 150
"… a certain Negro in the town of Nashville called Bobb be permitted to sell Liquor and Victuals…"

November 1797 – *Minutes of the Superior Court (Tennessee) p.205*
An assault case occurred at the "house of Black Bob"

May 1800 – *Minutes of the Superior Court (Tennessee) p. 317*
Schoolmaster Anderson Lavender indicted for assault "upon one black Negro man nam'd Bob." Andrew Jackson one of the judges

October 1801
Citizens of Nashville send a petition to the Tennessee General Assembly requesting the emancipation of Bob.

October 3, 1801 – *Journal of the House of Representatives*
"Also, the petition of sundry inhabitants of Davidson County, that a negro man named Bob be emancipated by act of assembly, &c. report, that same is reasonable and ought to be granted."

November 4, 1801 – *Journal of the Senate*
"The Senate took up the Bill to emancipate and set free a negro man called Bob. Ordered, that this bill be read, which being read was passed the third and last time, and ordered engrossed."

November 10, 1801 – *Fourth General Assembly of the State of Tennessee, Chapter XCIII*
"An Act to emancipate and set free a negro man named Bob...shall in the future be known as Robert Renfro."

June 1802 – Advertisement in *Tennessee Gazette*
Robert Renfro opens, "House of entertainment in the house adjoining Mr. Joseph M'Keans house. Necessary accommodations for man and horse."

August 1804, Deed "Searcy, Rentfro and Searcy
Robert Renfro obtains life estate in a portion of Lot #25

November 1805 – *Mero District Court of Equity, Nov. Term, p. 399*
Robert Renfro vs Charles Dickenson

1805 Superior Court of Law and Equity
King, Carson, and King vs Rentfroe
Rentfroe vs Dickinson

October 18, 1808 – Advertisement in *Clarion*
Robt. Renfro "continues to keep up his Boarding House as usual on Main Street at the sign of the Eagle."

February 21, 1811 – *Davidson County Deed Book "H", p. 44-5*
Robert Renfro to John McNairy and William Lyle, Jr. Pledges household goods, kitchen equipment furniture etc. to secure a loan.

1812
Robt. Renfro is #954 on Captain Cloyd's Militia Company.
Robert Renfro is on Davidson County tax list.

August-September 1812 – Advertisements in *The Democratic Clarion & Tennessee Gazette*
"…still occupies that convenient and noted stand on main street, Nashville, at the sign of the cross keys…"

March 15, 1814 – *Clarion and Gazette* account of March 11 fire.
"…could not save…the tavern house of Robert Rentfroe…"

March 23, 1814 — Advertisements in *Nashville Whig,* later appeared in *Clarion-Gazette*
"…his house burnt down in the destructive fire, and having since rented the stone tavern on the public square, near the courthouse…"

April 26, 1815 – Davidson County Court Minutes Vol. "K" p. 215-7
Robert Rentfro vs Richardson Tyre—Judgement for Rentfro, One cent.
Robert Rentfro vs Richardson Tyre and Rose Tyre—Judgement for Rentfro, One cent.
Robert Rentfro vs John Boyd—Judgement for Rentfro $100.

Jan. 1816 – *Davidson County Quarterly Minutes 1814-1816 Jan Session 1816 p.519*
Deed of lease between Robert Rentfro of the one part and Earnest Benoit of the other part…also a covenant here to attached between Wilkins Tannahill of the one part to Robert Rentfro of the other part… (NOTE: This is the last official record of Robert Renfro)

December 25, 1819 – Robert Searcy purchases Lot #25 and several other lots from James Trimble. No mention of Robert Renfro

1820 – Robert Renfro's name DOES NOT APPEAR:
United States Census of Nashville
ReServey of Nashville

Larry Michael Ellis

SIGNATURES ON THE EMANCIPATION PETITION

Page1
1. Richard Cross —*Operated House of Private Entertainment*
2. B. J. Bradford—*Newspaper Publisher – 2nd Mayor, 1809*
3. John Deatherage—*Furniture and cabinet maker - High Constable 1807*
4. Thom. Deatherage —*Furniture and cabinet maker*
5. Jno. Anderson—*Justice of the Peace 1802, City Recorder 1806, Bank Cashier*
6. William Carter
7. James King—*King, Carson & King Merchants*
8. Tho. Childress—*Kept the Bell Tavern*
9. J. A. Parker—*Tavern Owner*
10. William Lytle, Jr—*Land Agent -member of the Lavender jury*
11. Geo. B Curtis

Page 2
12. Wm Boyd
13. David Philips
14. Robt. Bustice
15. J.B. Craighead—*Merchant – son of the Presbyterian Minister*
16. Thom Childress, Sr.—*Co-founder Nashville Female Academy*
17. W. P. Anderson—*Attorney, friend of Andrew Jackson, founder of Huntsville, Ala.*
18. Patrick Lyons
19. Jacob Lovell
20. Robt. Currey—*Early Postmaster, Mayor 1822*
21. Wm Leary
22. Hennerey White
23. Jon Davis—*Justice of the Peace*
24. Tho Malloy—*Surveyor, Laid out the City of Nashville, Signed Cumberland Compact*
25. John Sample
26. William Turner
27. Charles T. Carson —*King Carson & King – Merchants*
28. J. Johnson

29. Jas. Hays
30. J. T. Elliston—*Silversmith – Mayor 1813*
31. Gideon Pillow—*Surveyor*
32. Oliver Johnson—*Merchant-Trader*
33. Wm. Hickman
34. R. Searcy—*Attorney, Legal owner of Bob*
35. Geo. S. Gray
36. E. Stout
37. Wm. B. Bell
38. S.... Cloyd—*May be Sarah Cloyd, a female property owner*
39. David Moore—*High Constable 1808*
40. George Bennet
41. T. Nicholas Roman (?)
42. J. H. Boyd—*Sheriff*
43. Francis McNairy—*Brother of Judge McNairy*
44. Thomas Talbolt—*Inn Keeper, Justice of the Peace*
45. Robt. Hewitt—*Justice of the Peace*
46. John Nichols—*Justice of the Peace*
47. John Weatherspoon—*Justice of the Peace*

Page 3
48. E Gamble —*Justice of the Peace*
49. Sam Weakley —*Surveyor*
50. Jno Dickinson—*Attorney*
51. John McNairy—*Judge – added a note, "provided this ..."*
52. Tho Crutcher—*Mayor 1819, Served as State Treasurer*
53. J. Coleman—*Attorney, Partner of Searcy, 1st Mayor*

Page 4
House of Representatives ....
Oct 1
Read & referred to the Com
Matters of Propositions & Grievances
                    Ed Scott, Clk

In Senate Oct 1, 1801
Read & referred as above
G. Roulston, Ck

Reported on_____

ABOUT THE AUTHOR

Larry Michael Ellis, a sixth generation Tennessean, was born and raised in Clarksville, Tennessee. After completing Clarksville High School in 1957, he served four years in the United States Navy before attending Austin Peay State College receiving a B.S. degree in 1965. He received a Master of Public Administration degree from Middle Tennessee State University in 1971. He was Director of the Tennessee Governor's Highway Safety Program for almost twenty years, serving four different Governors.

His love of Tennessee history spawned the writing of *Spizzerinctum, the Life and Legend of Robert "Black Bob" Renfro*. This is his first novel. Mr. Ellis has been married for 42 years and has three children and six grandchildren.

Printed in the United States
22696LVS00005B/1-9